ANITHA PADANATTIL

GIRL
IN A
MILLION

ROOM9 PUBLICATIONS

www.artoonsinn.com

Disclaimer: This is a work of fiction. Names, characters, businesses, places, events and incidents are either the products of the author's imagination or used in a fictitious manner. Any resemblance to actual persons, living or dead, or actual events is purely coincidental.

First Edition 2021

ISBN: 978-81-949824-0-1

Published by ArtoonsInn Room9 Publications, India
Printed in India by Manipal Technologies Limited, Manipal

ArtoonsInn Room9 Publications
www.artoonsinn.com

The words within are dedicated to the one person whose faith in my abilities has remained undiminished.

Ammae - my mother, this is for you.

Acknowledgements

Memories and experiences make you what you are and I thank them for it.

My thanks to the infinite source—the one that foresees everything and that includes, this little book.

A big thank you to my father - most reliable troubleshooter, for the unflinching support.

My thanks also go out to Mithru Rachamalla - Founder and CEO of ArtoonsInn for betting on Girl in a Million. Success follows the footsteps of the dreamers and the passionate. May your dreams continue to blossom and provide happiness to many.

Dearest Husnazi aka Husna Thaslim – editor and grammar Nazi, what would I have done without your timely insights? Thank you, from the bottom of my heart.

Khyati, your tireless support aided by a wonderful team at Room9 has been invaluable in bringing this book to life. Need I say more?

I would also like to express my gratitude to my friends, well-wishers and, members of the ArtoonsInn family for providing the daily dose of cheer. This has ensured that my bag is always cluttered with smiles and similar what-nots.

As for Sreesan V.B. whose wonderful illustrations helped in adding a special dimension to this book, I'm glad I always have him by my side.

'You are the Koteeswari. You are the Forcethinker.

Embrace the disparate and unfold.'

Sometimes, I shudder.
Shudder as I reflect.
On what might have been.
Was the back and forth worth all the trouble?
There used to be games that hurt and I flinch at the memory. The stings had been sharp. They had torn through until bits of them- the heinous ones, would ooze outwards to reveal me - make me visible. I was flawed, wasn't I? It was true and I knew it.

Then there was the despise. The taunts that reeked; all those failures, the mistakes, countless revisions, hours of hand-holding and the emotional racketeering. In the midst of all this, fragments of joy played peekaboo. The entry had been effortless. Such miniscule moments transformed me, gave me life and made me whole.

And through them emerged the fabric that constituted the real me. I had begun to take shape.
A coracle-style ride, slow and wobbly, awaited.
Seems like yesterday – this undulating path that I had traversed. Was this me? Truly me?

My thoughts are all over the place. Forgive me.
There are times when perception gets cloudy and the rambling tends to kick-start. Not at the moment though.

Often, most often, a chimera arises. It alternates between the scorched earth and three pairs of racing feet in various shades of brown. Feet encased in blue and white flip flops that have puffs of dust enveloping slender calves. Four pairs of eager hands clasping one other to form a rough circle. Soon, heads begin to toss outwards, curls bounce and plaits begin to unwind. Awkward shuffle gets into place and the familiarity of it all makes me smile.

Loving hands enfold me.
So gentle is the embrace that I gradually relax. The sensation
courses through until I finally let go.
To bask in the comfort that is on offer.
I am now safe, Core Z.
I feel safe.

PART I

Sagarika's Zenana

(Year 1986)

Ours was that exclusive zenana that had pimples and charred epidermis along with oil-laden plaits and armpits that could be smelled two classes away. A coterie of assorted spindly schoolgirls whose infectious charm created an instant buzz in school.

The 'Silver Flower Higher secondary School' located in *Oothukudi[1]*, *Koottupuram[1]* district was a novel one. Novel as in, English being given prominence instead of the local lingo—Thamizh. The ensuing rush resulted in a massive serpentine queue that stretched outwards of the thatched shed that belonged to the watchman of the school.

An entrance exam that determined how well each of the selected students proved their competence in the language, assured entry into the famed classrooms. This was where we all met for the very first time. In a class of sixty plus students, the five of us bonded over random assorted incidents and thus was formed a friendship that lasted several, several years. Coming to think of it, the school proved miraculous for us.

Studies were dismissed casually with a shake of our heads. I was the designated clown of the group who lived to entertain and defy orders. My life, my rules—was my passionate and fervent diktat and life couldn't be any simpler.

To me at first, the place we had landed in seemed quaint, non-social and vulgarly boring. Oothukudi, a name that I hated divulging to my friends up in the northeast, seemed to be a rudimentary place that simple persons inhabited. I therefore christened it *'Kanhaganj'*[1] informing one and all by way of letters and postcards, of its vibrant culture and quirky traditions. Kanha or little Krishna's fanciful life surrounded by friends and family was something I craved to be in. Therefore, I created my very own world, where laughter and gaiety ruled and that would make me the object of envy. I enjoyed the duplicity for a while and delighted myself in my fanciful illusionary world through which I received a sort of temporary happiness.

Soon enough, the illusion began to fade and the letters stopped coming. A slow breach had begun that infringed and transformed contrived perception into haze-filled pockets which were then secreted into designated nooks. These were cubby holes designed to hold in bits and pieces of myself. I realized that friendships of the long-distance kind, was a fickle emotion as it thrived and flourished on constant inputs. When one was immersed in day-to-day affairs, emotions were most often relegated to distant corners unless the dust was not allowed to settle over them in tiered layers. Efforts to revive old, established connections required time and patience… something, which most children would not deign to think or follow through. We were growing and experiencing life. Where was the time to think about matters that were not in the present? Fine dust thus settled and formed layers and we grew accustomed to the new and did not pause to think of the old.

Having been transported from the state of Assam in my case, to the small town called 'Oothukudi' in haste on account of my father's failed business ventures wherein his trusted friends cheated him out of his life savings, it was a difficult period of transition for all of us. I however failed to realize at the time that my parents and little brother were as affected by the change as I was and so, I found myself sinking into abject gloom on account of the shocking changes my system was being subjected to.

I attribute the Silver Flower Higher secondary School for transforming me into the person I am now. That, along with other nature-defying incidents, which contributed to the change, of course! All those months of brooding, sullenness, and silent anger dissipated slowly, chiefly because of the persistent efforts of Team Zenana. We looked out for each other. Our bond was genuine. Life was totally uncomplicated at that point of time. It was the best period of my life and despite all the highs and lows that I had been through, I still look back and thank the school for giving me one of the happiest times throughout the so-called 'dreaded' adolescent phase.

*

At first glance, pudgy Marge had me revolted. Her hawkish eyes behind the extra-large 'shell' framed spectacles looked me up most thoroughly as I squirmed in my seat and continued to etch out a noodle worm on the wooden tabletop with the tip of my Camlin compass. I sensed the continuous steely-eyed stare but refused to look up. The teacher droned on and commanded that notebooks be taken out. There was the familiar rustle of paper and the gentle thud of books falling onto the floor.

Meanwhile, I surreptitiously placed the notebook over my handiwork and proceeded to unscrew the lower half of my Hero ink pen. A prized possession in those days, I had received it from an uncle a few months ago as a birthday gift. It was a smuggled item, having been transported over the border by scraps that were the designated courier for pint-sized luxury goods. These impoverished children ran across the border just to make a living. When business was dull, they drove their cattle over to the other side for the day's graze or even worked in houses as temporary house help.

Dusk would find them back in their dimly lit mud homes, huddled beneath a solitary kerosene lamp where they would probably share a meager meal. Once the flickering tongue of light that strained through the soot filled glass would sputter and surrender to the darkness, the wild dogs roaming about outside would begin their cacophony. The incessant howling as they moved around would continue until the tiny pinpricks of light dotting the sky would fade from sight and the sky gradually lightened.

Espying Marge watching me with a bold eye, I lightly inclined the notebook with my left hand. With the right, I proceeded to fill in the etching with blue Camlin ink. The ink ran through the scarred wood, greedily covering up the spaces as I pressed the soft rubber syringe of the pen. So engrossed was I in the artwork of my making that I failed to notice Padmaja teacher approaching my desk.

'Tlinggggg' sang Marge's stainless steel lunch box as it spattered its mushy contents all over the floor. Marge had determined the sinister level of the situation quite approp-riately and had saved me from a possible caning that day and yes, I had thus chanced upon my first female bestie. She was bold and loud but did she ever take up the rap for me that day and every other day since then? Oh, yes. That she did and a lot, lot more. Our smart phone app calls us 'soul twins'. After all these years, how could we not be that?

*

I was a sucker for books. Rated a close second behind the primary passion was piling on the edibles, shoveling them in until the threat of regurgitation dawned. My accommodative esophagus had no say in the matter and was always put to the test yet, was game enough to hold on and prove its might. That apart, the tiniest scrap of paper merited a quick glance from my bug-sized eyes. Apparently self-taught and obsessed since the age of three-and-a-half, all that kept me attentive and interested were books. Dolls, dressing up, playing girlie games and all things feminine neither interested me nor helped rein in the fascination with all things wholesome and hearty. When a furious parent barred the traipsing of the outdoors, I would hole up with a new book devouring everything that was on offer. My mother spirited away magazines and instructed her friends to hide 'X' rated books under their mattresses. Though comprehension level was dim, I still managed sneak peeks at the contents primarily because they were not meant for my entertainment. The rebel heart in me did not allow for subservience.

It was hence, books of all shapes and sizes: the Amar Chitra Katha's, the Enid Blytons, the Hardy Boys and their ilk, the dictionary, film posters, folk tales, illustrated books from Russia, The Reader's Digest, magazines for children such as Sputnik, Target and Tinkle, lab manuals, glossy brochures, a distant cousin's college textbooks, the newspapers… anything I could lay my hands on, in any home that we visited, inevitably led me to the corner that beckoned and that was that! There were occasions when I would script out fanciful stories into my notebooks and the newness of the worlds I created, enthralled me no end. One in particular, lies nestled within the pages of my little red book and I think that you (the reader) would find it entertaining. It would be good fodder for young mothers with children who require constant engagement. Of course, you are at liberty to blow it out of proportion. The narration coupled with subsequent discussions should be a fun exercise anyway!

Unsurprisingly, the urge to pen down random thoughts proved to be exhausting. It was a tedious affair, the writing. I discovered that reading was far easier and enjoyable. As for the writing…. well, a labor of love was no fun if pleasurable pastimes were to be excluded from my profile. That coupled with several sets of prying eyes gradually deterred the creative urge within me.

May I have the temerity to mention here that Indian parents have deep-rooted systemic preferences? Their likes and dislikes and mindsets are well entrenched within the very same commonality. Whatever the cultural differences, the mind-set across generations remains unchanged. One word that would suit this condition best would be—herd mentality. Boys vs. girls, fair vs. the-not-so-fair, awesome grades vs. abysmal failures, well-heeled vs. the unfortunate and so on. Opinions are tossed around casually while the mild and the meek endure in silence. It was hoped that I would turn out to be a fair and demure child. A well-mannered doll face who would sing when asked to and speak well when spoken to. Since I loved being the rebel and persevered to be the exact opposite of who I was supposed to be, I suppose expectations were shattered. It gave me great inner pleasure to refuse to sing popular Bollywood numbers, both old and new and I loved to watch expectant faces crumble in the face of my outright refusal. The elders would shake their heads and leave me alone mortifying my mother. There were whispered discussions behind several sari-covered mouths about the unnecessary theatrics and behavioral issues considering the fact that I was already a performer of bhajans (devotional songs) at the All India Radio Station in Silchar, Cachar district, Assam. Being one of the youngest artistes at the station who could sing along with an on-the-spot improvised tune that the instrumentalists managed to piece through, it was a terrific feel to be affectionately carried about on the shoulders of the senior artistes afterwards. I could by then gauge accurately between moments of genuine happiness and all the poison-inducing barbs that hurt my mother the most.

Perhaps my observation of hypocritical behavior such as these resulted in the deep-rooted dislike towards any outward display of this gift of mine. I gradually stopped singing openly and hummed tunes in secret. Instantly picking up melodies regardless of the language and identification of the singers became a favorite past time. Most friends of mine knew that I sing a bit and I preferred to keep it that way. I tend to croak and cackle nowadays but have managed to pass on a few tips and tricks to some kids who I think could make the cut. How they utilize the pointers and put them to use are for them to choose and work upon.

We had hardly completed a month of active schooling when the section-wise indoor competitions were announced. There was essay writing, poster painting, light music, best handwriting and several other categories that enticed everyone to apply. I put in my name for the essay writing and light music category. None at home knew what I did in school. I merely came and went every day. Knowing my fondness for instant outbursts, mum always held the peace. She had my brother and her job as a primary school teacher to keep herself occupied anyway.

D-day dawned. We were called from our classes to the music room. The teacher sat cross-legged on the floor. I noticed the lack of a mike. It was going to be a face-to-face rendition thereby guaranteeing a hindrance-free creative output. New schools such as ours would invest in equipment at a steady pace as years go by depending on availability of resources. The obligatory name was called out and the one who completed his or her piece would be asked to leave. No loitering around to listen in. Curiosity of this sort would earn the wrath of the harridan.

Gayathri, the teacher's favorite, sang away. It was like listening to the female version of Shri Balamuralikrishna. What irked me was the fact that this being a light music competition, the song that was happening right there had classical inflections and variations similar to those of Carnatic *krithis*[5]. Watching the harridan smile and move her head to the vagaries of the tune, I felt my heart sink.

Weakly gesturing that a visit to the loo was a necessity, I scurried away from the room. It was as if a heavy load had settled on my slim shoulders. Having been the recipient of admiration for this long, I dreaded rejection. This was something that I was unaccustomed to. Warily making my way back from the filthy toilet, I glimpsed Shruthi leaning against the parapet wall, watching me. She watched my expression of disgust and smiled in sympathy. I had had to pick my way through piles of faecal matter that laced the toilet floor.

Water was a scarce commodity those days and the taps most often ran dry. But when you had to go, you just went about your business and the piles stank and grew in volume. It was only after the school closed that the ayahs made their appearance to clean out the muck. They were no better than the regular scavengers I suppose, being paid a pittance and overworked to boot. The cloying smell of phenyl would cloud one's senses but very soon, the fetid odor would fight for dominance. I had learnt to clear out my troubles most efficiently. How long was one to hold the breath and practice self-control? A battle-scarred veteran would find the going quite tough, I thought. I dreaded contracting a urinary infection but when resistance proved feeble and automatic relief seemed imminent, the choice was to rush along in a mad, blind run. I, therefore, emerged from the dimly lit cavern and pondered glumly on the upcoming battle that already seemed to be heading for a dismal loss.

I had judged Shruthi to be of the quiet kind. Since we hardly knew each other, I stood next to her with our backs supported by a low parapet wall while we watched the sun's rays play on the wall opposite us. She had turned her head and smiled at me. Shruthi had brown eyes, I noticed, and a kind smile. I remember her telling me, "You know…Gayathri is just a show-off. I have heard you hum and I know that you are way better than her. Don't you ever think that you can NOT do this. Whatever you have been in the past, I have no idea but this, I know. She is no match for you. Just let the teacher hear you." And that was how I fell for kind-hearted Shruthi. She had divined my dilemma and though she was not much of a talker, she could pack quite a punch when she did. Needless to say, I had had the harridan floored.

A short while later, Gayathri upped for the land of the trumpet. She now resides in the land of the whites, safely ensconced alongside her pupils. Shruthi had been right all along and with Marge for company, we made a fabulous threesome.

*

April 2017

[My thoughts suddenly flit back to the present. I seem to be alternating between my girly past and the more recent past. My apologies for the inconvenience but please do stay with me. You will get wind of the situation soon enough.]

I wake up.

And look at familiar surroundings.

However…. there's something different about today.

Wait a minute.

Is that the same clock on the wall?

It's what I asked for, I know. But it's not the same as the one in my bedroom.

Pause.

Refocus.

Think.

This is a hospital. My hospital.

I should know. I chose the wall colors. The shades and blinds in every room. Including the basic furniture.

So, why am I here?

My eyes turn to my right. I look at the IV tube connected to my arm.

Drip, drip.

On my left is my nephew Chandrashekhar, renowned Oncologist and, Director of the Sagarika Group of Charitable Hospitals. He has a concerned look on his face.

I smile at him and raise my eyebrows.

"It's nothing, so far," he responds. "You've had a minor fainting spell. We are running the tests."

Chandru gets up and walks over to the chart by the bedside. The question and answer session will begin now. I know the routine well enough. This is what I would do too. I sigh.

"Go on, Chandru," I say.

After we dispense with the initial queries, the probing begins.

"Since when have you had these episodes aunty Sagu?"

I chew thoughtfully on the insides of my cheek as the mind fumbled with a reply. Being evasive has never been my strong-point. But Chandru is known for his dogged persistence and I blurt out, "Not sure, Chandru. Didn't think of maintaining a record."

I have been quick on the uptake and Chandru suspects that for sure but mercifully enough, I am let off the hook.

I know when they began though.

They occurred a few days prior to Manu's take off on the quest for the unknown. The recurrences have been fairly frequent since then.

I have been terrified but maintaining the façade at home and work is a must. No point in letting people down. *A thing I learnt from a friend called Marge ages ago. That's aunty S for you.*

"Aunty, if you are not going to open up, I'll have to run some more tests."

I shrug. Nothing I cannot handle.

Chandru replaces the chart, gives an audible sigh and indicates that he has to leave. He motions at the clock, holds out three fingers, points at me and closes his eyes. I nod. This is how we communicate when we run out of words. He has been with me for quite some time now. My nephew and son—both rolled into one.

I drift off to sleep.

I dream of Assam. See it in my mind's eye; the lovely, unspoilt land of the Assamese. Of late night weddings under the full moon and houses enclosed within bamboo fences, the thatched mud huts beside paddy fields, impromptu picnics held in the mangrove a few furlongs away from home, running bare feet through freshly turned clayey soil looking for crayfish, of hopscotch games as well as lock and key madness, the mad tumble through gentle mounds of grass engaged in fierce fights with Manu, trading fisticuffs with the local lads and returning home with torn chemise and bloody knees.

My senses are on a high. I feel the warm tangy air. Memories of trips to school on the cycle rickshaw that is tipped on one side with heavy schoolbags and lunch boxes and crammed children on the other end with some of them awkwardly perched on a single buttock. Of the day that father came to pick us up on his Vespa scooter and realizing that the foul odor that pervaded my senses was actually my brother. He had done the potty in his shorts. Father's reaction to my awkwardness was to ride on blithely.

The memory makes me grin.

And grin turns to chuckle.

Ratna—short for Ratnalakshmi K. B.—looks at me and smirks. There's a part of me that has locked her inside. Tight. So tight, that I can see her grimace, nostrils expanding with the effort.

I was back within a setting that was familiar and close to my heart. The white walls with the blue bordered windows of our classroom offered scant comfort as I squirmed on receiving the 'sure shot backward ankle kick', a Ratna-special. My toes curled in response as exquisite pain flooded my being and my eyes watered mightily. I heaved a deep breath and summoned my resources. I knew that the action had been made to convey annoyance over our constant chatter. Sitting just ahead of me gave her the clean angle she needed. The effect of the kick was such that it took a few hours for the pain to subside. I was furious and vengeful. She needed to feel my S tackle—and soon. It was primarily a rules-free contest that depended on how fierce the participants were. As I fumed and waited for recess to begin, Malini rushed up to me and said, "Don't try any stuff with her, S."

The champion in me rose ten feet higher. Scared was she?

"Actually, quite the opposite. It's just that she has an artificial right limb."

Marge, Shruthi and I, we were floored. Now where did that come from? Malini indicated that Ratna was walking over in our direction and hurriedly disappeared into the crowd.

I watched her amble towards us. She wore the same but slightly crumpled uniform and a similar set of canvas Bata shoes like all of us. Nothing marred her complacent expression. Her gaze though, was locked on me—direct and unwavering.

"Hello, S. You seem to be quite popular. I'm Ratnalakshmi K.B. Are we friends?"

String of words recited without pause.

She had planned it well and I had to hand it to her.

Three solemn pair of eyes inspected the intruder. Ratna's knowing chuckle triggered the first of our uproarious laughter sessions.

That was our Ratna; unapologetic, yet sincere. Our rock. I wouldn't want her to lose her composure for any nincompoop situation. Ever.

She stayed in the student quarters the school had just built. It was reserved for children who were deemed special cases. Physically challenged was not a word we used then. She was a bit slow, gait wise. Plus the fact that she spent her holidays in each of our homes practically made her a family member. Not having a mother and having been raised in various hostels from a very early age, made her appreciate the love and concern of the mothers towards their progeny. Some-thing that was so casually taken for granted by us strengthened her resolve to firmly point out facts reducing the guilty member to a squirming mess of tears and penitence. Not surprisingly, our mothers adored Ratna. And she, in turn, basked in the warmth.

So here we were: Zenana's core.
- With Marge – my soul twin,
- Shruthi – the Buddha with the punch,
- Ratnalakshmi K.B. – space within my heart,
- Malini – on-and-off entrant and lastly,
- Yours truly – most vulnerable goof!

I do not know why I always likened core Z to the curry of South India, the ubiquitous Sambar. Its tangy aroma enticed me from any hole that I crawled into, books be damned. I could mop it up with any kind of bread, scoop it up with my palm and gulp it down. Any remaining rivulet would be licked all the way from my elbows to the tip of my fingers. Secretly licking the plate clean was another passion of mine. Wrathful looks and tight slaps I would deal with later.

I transferred this liking to my BFF's calling Marge, the dhal of my life. Shruthi was the roasted, ground coconut that could knock me senseless with her one-liners. Ratna, my spicy darling, spread her somberness through her flavors. Malini was the sour tamarind juice that might or might not be needed for the recipe on that particular day. And I was the seasoning, the grand dame that topped the delicacy and announced to everyone assembled that here was the flavorsome manna, ready to be served.

Seasonal vegetables were added as per availability and these formed the next level of the Z. Thus, we had sambar with tomatoes, sambar with small onions, sambar with drumstick, sambar with white or, red pumpkin pieces, sambar with carrots and potatoes, sambar without tomatoes and so on… a seemingly endless concoction that could be recreated over and over again. Friends would pop in according to the occasion and stay in for a temporary period. Friendships ranged from a week to several months. There were no hard feelings. Every newcomer was welcomed and absorbed into the general melee. Leave takings went as per what the situation entailed. It was, therefore, a good series of uncomplicated summers.

*

Unseen hands grope
Grapple and seek.
They fight their way through the darkness.
Terror engulfs me.
Screams bubble in my throat.
I try to shrink. Meld into the shadows.
But the hoarse voice continues to whisper.
Urges me to remain still.
Helpless tears flow.
No one hears me. No one knows.
Therefore, I remain.

Boxed up in a distant fragment within me, I shake uncontrollably at the memories and wake up gasping.

The shivering continues. It is primal. Submerged deep within, but one that threatens to resurface from time to time.

I clench my fist and close my eyes. Summon my maker.

Chandru finds me in this trance-like state. He waits by the door, anxious. When my eyes open, I register his presence. He is immediately by my side.

"What was it, Aunty Sagu?"

"Just a nightmare, Chandru. The usual. Don't worry about it."

"Do you want to talk about it? If not with me, Dr. Hema would be glad to help out."

"At this stage? Don't think that would be necessary," I reply smilingly. "They have a limited time span, same as everything else."

Chandru doesn't enjoy this flippancy. He's always been the sober one. After a grunt that conveys dissatisfaction, he leaves the room.

I gesture towards my smartphone. It's been a while since I checked in. A nurse admires the ink blue personalized cover and respectfully hands it to me. Within seconds, I'm engrossed.

Block it, box it up and shift to an enjoyable pastime, Sagarika. This will pass. It always will.

All those mountains that have been climbed… it's time for succor. Gently herald in the shift - tiny voices chime on the sly.

Heaven help me but I'm not done yet.
So, crawl back to your corner. You, the harbinger of ill will.
Just stay where you are.
Stay!

*

[Meanwhile, getting back to the zenana…]

We borrowed bicycles for the lunch hour trip, four Butterbee bicycles. Ratna was perched behind Marge. None of us could handle the extra weight. The handle wobbled but Marge managed to plod on.

Exit slip requirement was a rarity those days. A casual request to the class teacher followed by her nod of acquiescence would suffice. Plans would be made beforehand and a trip to a friend's house for lunch, stationary shop for greeting cards, the nearby library or even the ice-cream shop for a refreshing summer treat would be made. Ogling at boys and getting ogled in return heightened the sense of achievement.

Skin crimping in the merciless sun, sweat breaking out all over followed by damp patches under the arms and backs, bushy eyebrows and hairy upper lips nonetheless, our giggles and covert glances clothed in blue pinafores attracted furtive stares. Unwanted comments and leers were left for the kind attention of Deendayal, Marge's brother. Watching him caress bruised knuckles with pride enmeshed us even more into the snug cocoon we were in. It seemed to us as if we were in our own secret little world.

Tests and exams flew by. Two summer vacations were spent at Oothukudi and life seemed to be settling down. Malini seemed to be even more elusive. A covert bird whispered that she was 'carrying on' with a salesman from the swanky shop down the road. Marge and Shruthi tried to knock some sense into the girl. But it seemed to me that a different light had entered her eyes.

Enamor was a word, an emotion I had read about. But hurting the family and us, resisting caution, being reckless and gay was a side of Malini we had never been exposed to. She seemed lethargic, gazing dully out of the windows on some days and on others, humming romantic Thamizh melodies. Malini and romance was an unusual combination that had us dumbstruck, flabbergasted.

The covert bird once again informed us that Malini had upped to Tirupathi with her beau. This, she informed, was to exchange garlands in the presence of the Lord and enter the hallowed portals - blissful wedlock was our surmise.

Our wrath knew no bounds and off we flew on the borrowed bicycles to Malini's house. We felt our courage desert us as soon as we spied hordes of concerned people assembled in a large group outside the house and scrambled for a quick getaway but our bikes were confiscated and the questioning began soon after. After a while, we managed to convince them of our innocence in the matter and were allowed to leave by the troubled family members. Loud discussions were held as to whether the police should be informed. Lamentations against the same were heard from within the house. Those could have quite possibly come from Malini's mother and the women of the house.

Feeling sick at heart and saddened at the turn of events (Ratna in particular), we made our way back to school. There was up roar over our absence. Classes had already begun—informed our friend, the kind-hearted watchman. And so, we trooped wearily to the Principal's office. Relating the events to the beady-eyed lady, we were dismissed with a curt warning and asked to hand in a written apology to the terrified class teacher who was being consoled by her colleagues in the staff-room.

But our eyes were blank and our hearts, heavy. What was to happen to Malini? Would she come back to us? Was she really and truly married? She had not completed her schooling. Wasn't that necessary? Why were we excluded from her private mooning sessions? Or did we just not notice or care? Ratna's face turned pinched and drawn. We were called for and question-ed by all the teachers. Some were kind. Some persistent, while most others remained unconvinced. We visited the store to ask about Malini but the manager kept shooing us out.

Our Zenana had shrunk. We felt depleted, helpless. The school however, remained and Oothukudi stayed in place. So we tried to meld in. No matter what, the days pretty much flew past us.

*

"She's fine. Fit as a fiddle," pronounced the Doctor to the grave faces assembled around him.

"At this age, the healing is faster. Repair processes, quicker," he mumbled. The elders squirm in their chairs.
Fine. Fit. Healing well.
Words.
Words.
Words!

An inner fiddle plays inside – grim reminder,
Of the ache that had burrowed deep within
Of a hurt that will carry on.
Loss of the tiny soul. That's on me.

I remain impassive though my innards shriek. I cringe in shame and guilt.
Soul. Tormenting. Grief.

My penance remains complete to this day.

To remain childless is not just an obligation…it is my *dakshina*[6]. To the lost one. For the one that I once had and did not, no, could not protect.

My stature within the family is complete. No one questions me about anything anymore. None would dare suggest anything with an iota of condescension.

What I do now, would be something that gifts me peace.

Everyone, do let me be.

The vile and the base have to give way to the fresh. Sagu is now S. My new cloak needs to be visited quite often and the familiarity woven through in dense layers.

Malayapuram, I had abandoned without a thought. Abandoned my hearing-impaired grief-stricken Ammumma. I could not, would not, return to my beloved Oothukudi as well. My beloved Z would visit me from wherever they were stationed.

My heart knew that. But for now, there was not a soul I yearned for. I did not need anyone…only, a fresh hole to crawl into. For as long as it took.

Flashes of a train ride and a yellow board that displayed the name-Koottupuram popped up. The first tear dripped down. And they wouldn't stop. I cried for two inescapable days. My sorrowful mother gave me company. I was inconsolable. My childhood, the Z, all the happiness, Oothukudi, were lost to me.

Systematically destroyed. My motto for life had been ripped out as I caved in to the desolation. I wept until exhaustion took over. Having been sleep deprived for long, numbness washed over and acted as painkiller.

For how long or how many days I slept, I do not remember. But when my eyes opened, I saw Marge, Ratna and, Shruthi.

My eyes welled as they scrambled towards me. Hugs turned into tears. Tears turned into smiles.

They were anxious.

I was relieved.

*

[Memories wash over me unceasingly and I surrender to the flow. I find that I have no control over my emotions that are in a state of tangled disarray. My thoughts sway from the past to the new perhaps, as a measure of solace. The pattern will be discerned through the randomness—it is what I can hope for. That, along with bytes interjected by members of the erstwhile zenana…. things should make sense soon enough!]

It was the season of the thunderstorms. I loved the gusts of wind followed by pouring rains. Blue… deep-blue mountains out yonder topped by misty wraiths. One could look out the window and revel in the beauty of nature all day. In the evenings when calm prevailed, long winding walks with Ratna along half-paved roads and quick visits to the homes of numerous aunts and uncles where we were welcomed with steaming cups of tea and assorted snacks. Stuffed and fried dumplings were what we preferred but we gratefully accepted whatever was on offer.

Those heavenly days at Sujata akka's home that were spent listening to music, reading, watching Doordarshan channel on TV and of course, gorging on rice and red bean curry accompanied by bite sized chicken coated with akka's special sauce. Her lentil soups and flavored mutton curries were lip-smackingly delicious.

Salvation comes in small doses.
Measured, but just right.
It takes funny twists and turns yet,
It is always there for you
When you need it the most.

Nilgiris. The Blue Mountain—my summer salvation for when I needed it the most.

With Ratna and Sujata akka in the lap of Ma Prakriti (Sanskrit for Mother Nature), I was in the charming city of Ootacamund lovingly called Ooty by the natives.

Sometimes, I wonder at the coincidence. Oothukudi, Koottupuram, Ootacamund. Could that be measured salvation? Chips of happiness cunningly dropped here and there to add to the charm?

Relief washed over me and Ratna sensed it. She was far too astute but refrains from questioning. We did not discuss the abstinence from the annual Malayapuram visit. My insistence on accompanying Ratna to her sister's home had a deeper reason but she knew better than to probe. We clung on to our childish prattle. Money was scarce but happiness was not. Seeking solace in the comfort of their understanding, I stored the secret box deep within the recess I had carved out.

Learning is a continual process. Of times spent in Assam, the music, Oothukudi and the zenanaiites, and now, Ootacamund. I learnt to accept the slow with the dull, tinged with a pinch of gaiety.

Happiness came and went. Everything was transient. Except for Malayapuram. The dull throb inside of me turned to pounding. Sweat broke out, drenching me, leading to sleepless nights.

I had to talk. How, was the question and, to whom. The when and the where mattered as well. This was my gallivanting dilemma that nibbled away at the innards.

Block it. Box it up, Sagarika. Another year bestowed. Salvation will provide. Keep the faith.

Ratna seems to be calling me. I have to pack up. Time to face the upcoming academic year.

Our ride back on a jolting state transport bus was uneventful except for the vehicle swerving around a hairpin bend. The feel of someone leaning on me set my teeth on edge. I crept closer and gripped Ratna's hand.

"You are seriously messed up, aren't you?"
For a fraction of a second, our glances coincide after which we hastily look away.

"Just come back to us...wherever you go." There was a catch in her voice.

I felt a tremor in me, felt the tears gathering. It took more than a superhuman effort to act normal after that. Our thoughts kept us silent for the remainder of the trip. Getting down at the bus depot, bags retrieved, we faced each other awkwardly. Ratna had done me a huge favor and she understood that. I hugged her tight. She was gracious. That girl. She squeezed me briefly and turned to board the bus to school. Mine was in the far corner...gears churning, and I hurried to get in.

We would meet again tomorrow.

That would be another bridge to cross.

I was safe until the next summer—dearest salvation, gracious bestower.

So I smiled, and waved at Ratna.

*

Rivulets of rain splatter on windowpanes. They are everywhere. In school, our homes, dribbling over the Pallavan Transport buses, the glass facade of the latest motorcycle showroom in Koottupuram, the trees and roads. The incessant downpour has filled up all the potholes and ditches and extinguished the fires at a nearby cemetery. We watch the spires of smoke funneling upwards through the wet glass panes of the bus and connect the moisture droplets with our fingers to form figures or names, anything that made sense. On occasions, blowing a hot breath of air and penning short notes on the patch thus formed, kept us amused until it was time to disembark.

Rushing to the main bus depot to collect our monthly bus tickets, jostling in the queue and scrambling to book seats next to the open windows was another after school once-a-month routine. Letting the wet spray wash over our faces and uniforms, hair dripping, shoes squelching and wet feet in socks nonetheless, our happiness remained firmly ensconced in the myriad pleasures of life.

Bad grades? No worries. The trick was to aim towards the finish line and not shed tears over minor obstacles. Marge wanted to dabble in stocks. Ratna wanted to be a professor. Shruthi aimed to be an ophthalmologist. As for me, I had not decided as yet. Give me a book, some music and good food and, I was done. I would prefer to get married to a chef who had a huge library. That would be my idea of the perfect haven – provided I got married!

Those were the childish dreams and aspirations dreamt by uncluttered, free minds. While some were achieved, others changed over the course of time to form new associations and newer ventures. Many died out or were abandoned. Intersecting unforeseen situations that created random patterns thus overlapping the old and the new. Whether destiny or fate, eventually the essence of salvation seems to be interspersed and woven into events forming a tapestry that becomes part of the whole. What seemed to be the end, turned out to be the beginning. Perspective over what is right and wrong seemed to border a thin divide. Nothing seemed good or bad anymore.

'The trick was to aim towards the finishing line and not shed tears over minor obstacles.'

I remembered that line. How relevant it seems even today.

Glow in the dark, glowworm. Your light might be snuffed out tomorrow. But today, it exists.

*

Vivid memories of the science laboratory disaster stood out. A harrowing time it had been for all of us. In a space packed with sixty odd students, equipment and reagents were never enough. Sharing was the common practice. Oftentimes, the ratio was three students or more to one equipment. We were seen huddled around the Bunsen burners, tuning forks, distilling and measuring apparatus, reagents both colored and noxious. There was a single point of exit should a calamity occur. Our teacher doubled up as the lab guide and assistants were scarce. Being organized solely rested on the principle of chaotic management. How we managed then, was and still is, a mystery.

A shriek drew us to the center of the room. Students had hurriedly moved over to the sides and Rani became the sole focus of our attention. The back of her pinafore was charred and dotted with holes. Her long plait was lying on the ground where the acid from the test tube had splashed through. The girl was whimpering and shivering in fear. Our poor teacher had run out for help. It was sheer luck that the acid content was miniscule and had spattered over Rani's back. The severity of the burns was hence, quite minimal. The horror of the situation and the gravity of what-could-have-been stared at us right in the face.

Rani was sent home and she rejoined school after a week, hair styled in a short bob. We surrounded her and she was overwhelmed by the attention. Our Principal conducted a special assembly and called her onto the stage. Her bravery in the face of adversity was commended. The hoopla over the incident soon faded away and school routines took precedence once again.

Splashes of the acid on the sides of the scarred desk attracted my attention. It reminded me of the termite-ridden channels made in the wooden columns and door ends of our Malayapuram house. The red mud would be meticulously scraped away, the wood sand papered and varnished but the eruptions would be spotted yet again, in another part of the stately home. The problem, it was said, rested in the foundation. Whatever had to be done, required ministration at core levels to contain the infestation. *How would an outer cleansing ensure closure of the rot that had already begun from deep within?*

I colored the damage on the desk with the blue ink of my pen. Delicacy in artistic endeavor calls for dedication and patience. It took me minutes stolen from several sessions to complete the layout. I named it, 'Root beard' with Rani's name and year etched out next to it. It was a minor sensation and offered a few more days of relevance to her. Petite Acid-Rani, who had had a miraculous escape.

*

My reveries are cut short. Duty calls. An array of ledgers, receipts and other items are brought to my attention. Thirumalai, our chief accountant waits by the door hesitantly. I motion for him to enter. We discuss necessities.

Time flies. I suddenly feel dizzy. The nurse, being quick to comprehend ushers everyone out of the room and Dr. Chandrashekhar is called for.

I lie down and my vital signs are being monitored. Chandru hurries in. I feel weak and irritated. This won't end. I need to be home. Look at my plants. Talk to the trees. Let them comfort me. I'm sure they miss me. It's been awhile.

I breathe in the scent of the jasmine flowers. The mild pungent *neem*[2]. Crush a leaf of the guava and lime plant between my fingers and inhale the aroma. Feel the rough bark of the *mangifera indica*[3], bestower of the sweet *Neelam*[4]. I look up to see the tall heads of the coconut palm sway in the breeze. My throat thirsts for the sweet water of the tender coconut. I want to walk barefoot on the grass, feel the rough sand and the gravel dig into my feet.

My train of thought shifts to the sounds of laughter. I hear the sounds of splashing water and the delighted gurgles. Of ice-cold water meeting skin and the resultant squeals. We had cowered beneath the thatched shed overhanging the pond. While Ratna watched, the three of us clad in our white singlets took turns, paddling dog-like, making short forays towards the center of the pond and back towards where she sat. There was a single bar of soap for our use. We rubbed it all over, paddled again and dried ourselves. Our dresses were randomly pushed through the narrow slats of the sloping thatched roof. With our backs turned towards each other and Ratna's eyes discreetly covered with the help of her palms, we changed into dry clothes in a rush. Afterwards, we scrambled up the loose sand and made a mad dash for the back entrance holding our dripping clothes in one hand. Washing the sand off our feet at the tap placed next to the steps leading to the house, we avoided the nips of the friendly stray tied to the pillar and ran in. Ratna ambled in after us, gently swaying with a smile.

Warmth, smiles, bonding. It feels strange to remember the heady days. The rush of relief that is associated with the beginning of the end.

The Zenana had tried. Made a brave effort. But we were naïve and naivety is a tangible thread that is as fragile as the hands that try to hold on.

*

Recollections of Marge

I vividly remember Sagu. I noticed her in her shorts skipping behind her father on the first day as we waited patiently to collect the application form for admission to the new school. I figured that she was an odd one. She hummed to herself and was oblivious to all the curious stares. An eighth grader was obliged to 'behave'; especially, a South Indian eighth grader. We were not kids anymore. But Sagu, she was different.

While we wrestled over tricky words and managed to complete our initial test paper put together by the new schoolteacher, Sagu had already rushed through the same in half the time and left for home with her parent. Since I kept a watch on her goings-on, I realized that she was quick. I wished to know her better. Her help during times like these would be extremely beneficial and a veritable time-saver for someone as non-studious as I was.

My resolve to get to know her strengthened especially from the time we were grouped together. I chose a seat diagonally ahead of her and was thus able to watch what she did in class. She was quite amusing. Most times whilst the teacher spoke, she would be engrossed in a book that was placed on her lap. Her rough book was the subject of several scribbles—weird patterns of blue and gray; ink blue and pencil-lead-tipped shades of gray filled the pages. Her text-books were not spared either. On and on she sketched with smudged fingers that had nails bitten through and along the sides.

At times, I got the feeling that she disliked everything around her... us, the school, Oothukudi. It seemed to me that she had flown in from a different world. Like Tarzan and his son Korak. They felt out of place in the city too, didn't they? The original misfits. Same as her.
Aliens cast into different spaces.

*

She did not know the local language and that proved to be irksome. We didn't know hers either and our usage of English was just basic anyway. However, I waited. I am known to be patient. This queer creature would be my friend. I wanted that badly as I felt deep down that she was special.

Opportunity presented itself one sunny day. Her habit of sketching in books shifted to a different medium. This time, the wooden desk she was using caught her fancy. I knew that she caught my gaze but chose to ignore it. As she scratched and worked on the upper corner of her desk, I secretly became her look eye. It was as she began coloring her creation that trouble loomed. Espying the teacher making her way through the nest of tables, I grabbed my lunch box and let it fall.

Gooey contents splattered all over the floor and pandemonium ensued. The teacher hesitated and hurried to my side. Girls scrambled towards the front of the class cooing in disgust. I had my ear mercilessly boxed and the ayah was called in to clear up the mess. I rubbed my sore ear and stole a look at Sagu. She had hastily cleared her act and caught my gaze. Our suppressed smiles confirmed what I had set out to do. Sagu was my first best friend from that day.

In many ways, Sagu seemed like a misfit. The girl hummed in Hindi. But, she was South Indian.

I had a half Telugu–half Tamil origin. So, Hindi was a no-no.

She had a 'Diana' cut. My curly hair was always braided.

She had inquisitive eyes. Mine were short sighted.

She read a lot but never seemed to read schoolbooks. I pored over the latter and never seemed to make much headway.

For her, exams were a breeze. She had decent grades, well enough for me anyway. I don't think she cared much about them. I was relieved to have an easy time with her around though.

There was some kind of trouble, the financial kind I gathered as her fee payment kept getting delayed during the first year. Things settled down apparently once her parents started regular work. Intimate matters concerning one's home were seldom discussed. Our activities and conversations almost always revolved around matters related to the school.

Ratna and Shruthi joined us and I was delighted to show them around Oothukudi. We visited all the stationary shops in and around school. Our bicycle rides took us to each other's homes. The ride to Sagu's was the longest and the house was always locked up. Her neighbor, an elderly pensioner, would hand over the keys to us and we would sit and drink something cool, lock up and be on our way.

A visit to my home was an event by itself. All my friends would be awed at the spread that awaited them. We would gorge on different kinds of rice and curries, savory snacks, cool juices and end up listening to Ilayaraja and Michael Jackson's songs on tape. Mom being an asthmatic would relax in her room under the fan and my brother Deendayal would keep an eye on us from the other room. He was elder to me by eight years and seemed stern and rigid to my mates. That was just a cover. In reality, Deenanna was a large hearted softie. He was our umbrella. The one who looked out for us. Gentle giant with the bony knuckles. Those punches connected quite well.

It was only once that the knuckle routine backfired. And how! Gross miscalculation cloaked in the garb of childishness. The regret has remained in us until today. A fistula of deep guilt lying in our gut that refuses to let go.
The umbrella that failed to offer respite…. wilting in the face of nature's fury. Our Sagu. Beloved zenaniite. How mightily we failed you.

*

(Sagu's Recount) 1990 –

The Year of Aimlessness

When you are seared, physical pain precedes the emotional. Slowly, as the numbness begin, the sense of 'being' in the real fades. The world around you narrows down so much so that the stark reminder, of having to cross an insurmountable obstacle - the one that looms ahead, remains. Save for the reservoir that builds and gathers, no other being can help tide over the mountain that only YOU are required to cross. It is either crossed or, the purpose remains defeated. It is as simple as that.

After the incident, we moved to the city. Relocation was painful. Everything was. What was not? A degree of pain is associated with any experience. Every experience would have that bittersweet flavor. Father's new job and my mother's lack of it, my brother's new school, the skipping of my board exams and of course, being far…far away from familiar surroundings. We were all in our holes. Digging deep. Trying to crawl through and cover ourselves from the eyes of the world.

No one suspected. None knew. But to us, we were the accused. The ones who carried the burden of guilt. Of shame. Each immersed in their private grief. Living listlessly. Trapped in limbo.

Books were forgotten. So was music. Home was not home anymore. There was a heavy cloud of suppression that gathered and darkened but did not burst open.

After a few months, it was decided that I would travel to Alappuzha, the land of the houseboats and rippling waters, with my mother. It was hoped that recuperation of the body and mind might be attained. But what of the soul, I wondered? Of the unseeing eyes that looked away. Silent, bitter, unyielding.

Hours were spent by the lagoon…contemplating. Watching the boats drift by. Fishermen working with their nets. The strange child was noted and commented upon. Did she speak the local language? Friendly passers-by drifted towards me and tried to strike up a conversation. Did I go to school? Was I sick? Did I have a family? I chose silence. The most effective tool. The light in my eyes had faded and that proved to be a deterrent. Slowly, I was left alone. Alone, to mull within my own thoughts.

I was made the butt of their jokes. Compared to *Kurinji*[13] who lived under the frangipani tree next to the well, a frangipani blossom tucked above her ear and curly unkempt hair streaked with dreadlocks, abstract mannerisms and clothes that reeked of piss, I could easily pass off as her younger self. Cruel jibes that should have hurt, yet, did not. They popped off me just like the darts that bounced off dartboards. In fact, I loved listening to the coarse taunts and abuses that accompanied the filthy language. I felt no curiosity at meeting Kurinji, my nemesis. She was in her own private hell I assumed, same as I.

My poor mother was at her wits' end. Unable to reach out and desperation reaching critical levels, I was forced to meet the Wise One on the recommendation of the locals. Something would come by. That was their solemn assurance.

*

Margie

(continued)

Pesky bright buttons. Those were her eyes, the ones that sparkled. The things I could glean from those eyes…. oh, what mischief they carried! Sagu remained the life and soul of our group. Bit by bit, the transformation was complete. The language was learnt. She was corrected and rebuked for failing to use respectful words. Murugan, the school watchman, became her tutor. She spent time with him and he in turn, became her ardent fan. So enamored was he of Sagu that he called her *Sagupaapaa*[8], his little one.

A day away from school entailed worried checks by Murugan following which, a quick after-school trip to her home ensued. Sagu's family welcomed him and he soon turned into a regular visitor. Murugan was apparently a son of the soil. And that was how he came to take charge of their little garden which soon teemed with ornamental plants in the front, fruit trees at the sides and a tiny kitchen garden lush with herbs and assorted vegetation in the backyard.

Sagu spent hours with him, honing her new skill. In turn, she taught him rudimentary English. Master now became student and received sharp rebukes from the young teacher. Sagu's mother upon watching Murugan's consternation, often reprimanded his impudent tutor and asked her to be patient with him as he was unlettered. To Murugan, however, his 'paapaa' did nothing wrong. After all, he needed to be perfect. So, he smiled and grinned along with her in all happiness.

Two summers passed in this delightful manner. It was a period of happiness and shared bonding. We were required to choose the stream that would decide our future career. I chose Humanities, as I did not want any subject that was too stressful. I would make sense out of it once I was out of school. I would consider the share market perhaps? Time was a precious commodity to us. We would be in separate divisions by the next academic year and that by itself was an unthinkable option.

Ratna and Sagu chose the science stream. Ratna was focused while Sagu was not. She chose science, as she did not want to be saddled with me. Ratna was not meddlesome and was quite independent so she would be free to pursue her interests apparently. Shruthi selected the home science option. She would be a good homemaker. Ophthalmology, she realized required a lot of effort and dedication, which was not her forte. We visualized her home; a happy one, with good food, laughter and contentment. The perfect wife and the ideal mother. That would be our Shruthi.

Never in our wildest dreams did we imagine our Sagu, to be running an independent organization. Sagu, of the childish laughter and constant companion, would turn out to be Doctor S one day. That she would be loved and revered by all was an unassailable belief. But to be looked upon as the epitome of efficiency, was an incomprehensible thought.

How times change!
How the tides turn!
What we plan, is not what is meant to be.
Yet, what we were yesterday, matter little to the one we are today.
Whom we think we know, has changed to someone unfamiliar.

*

The Bend is in Sight

Joining the endless queue that led to a small mud-tiled hut, I felt something stir in me. Something that was akin to curiosity. Watching families young and old, the squalling children, people with troubles writ large on their brow murmuring away, with gossip and animated discussions on just about every topic under the sun such as religion and the Wise One, the revered one's family and their connections, the weather, one's job, income and expenses of everyone concerned, conjecture, rivalries, state of the city, politics, animal husbandry, Kurinji and me etc., endless were the topics that were debated upon. My mother blanched and cringed. I was fascinated by the varied hues in her complexion as she eavesdropped shamelessly.

There was the long wait within the compound of the house and another interminable squat in the long open verandah. Jostling for space, I craned my neck to look in, as the door was ajar. A twinkling pair of eyes met my gaze. Taken aback, I looked away. As we neared the room I looked in once again and observed an entire wall covered with the pictures of deities. The man himself, clad in a white *veshti*[8], was reed thin and had scrawny gray hair. Sweat coursed through his body thereby explaining the discarded shirt within the small room. His smile widened on watching me observing him as he nodded at my mother. While he listened through her litany, I shut them out preferring to look outside instead. Did the sky turn a deep blue and the tulsi (basil) plant in the central courtyard a shade too green? I shifted my focus on the persons just outside looking at us, waiting for their turn. Could it be this simple then, to dump one's baggage? To receive the much needed respite? Was this the place that offered solutions for salvation? Temporary salvation! Never mind the sweat and the heat. Amazement coursed through me; at the realization that measurable hope could be rendered by a single person.

I turned and watched my mother speak. The Wise One grinned and uttered a single word, *'Koteeswari'* – girl in a million. My mother's flow of words halted and she looked at me thunderstruck. I remained calm. Unsmiling. Watched the camphor being lit. Accepted the proffered lemon. I felt the tremor in my mother's body as she folded her hands in obeisance and bent low, forehead touching the floor. The Wise man's piercing glance fell over me once again after which, he bent sideways to allow the next fervent devotee to tumble in.

We made our way back, down the rickety lane. Back to our rented one-roomed flat. My mother kept a tight hold of my hand. We were silent. Immersed on our thoughts. Efforts to initiate a conversation with me were always rebuffed. It was as though I was punishing her. In reality, I was punishing myself. For not trusting in them, not opening up. Perhaps, they could have halted what was to have happened. Instead, I brought them down to this. It was me, all along. Yet, they nurtured. Tried to kindle the flame. I was their precious first-born. The one who had bought in the magic. I had always known their love.

"This is not a disease, my child," she had told me with brimming eyes. "It will pass. You'll see."

"Let it go, my baby. Just throw it away and come back to us."

Hopelessness welled. I had hurt everyone close to me. Dare I dream again?

Feeling suffocated, I rushed out. Walked to my regular spot. Sat down to watch the still waters. Yet another day would pass in this manner.

*

Shruthi

April 1990

We were thrilled. The cat was finally out of the bag. And so, we were making our trip to Malayapuram with Sagu dearest, to meet her Ammumma - the family matriarch.

We had offered her our support. In fact, we were bristling with it. In another bogie sat Deenanna with two of his pals. He had agreed to come. One last favor just before he joined duty in Pune. The two groups agreed that utmost secrecy was to be followed. Deenanna and Co. would stay close to the home and not at the Malayapuram house. Our plan was on being around for three days. In fact, the return tickets were already booked. Sagu would stay back with her parents of course. She was happy and that mattered to us.

It was the perfect trip. The stately home with its many rooms sat amidst two medium sized ponds on either side surrounded by cashew, mango, drumstick, guava, jackfruit and, coconut trees and lush bamboo foliage framing the eastern border of the property. A tiny rivulet ran through the front of the house and we would be absorbed in the silver fishlings and sparkling waters merrily rushing through. Sagu's uncle stayed close by with his family and he visited the home twice every day. Meeting his mother was mandatory. Watching the siblings converse with their mother left us reeling. Sagu's mother and her uncle discussed events with the ease of long practice. Their hands, eyes and mouths synchronized as they pointed and prodded at each other to emphasize what they wished to convey. Sagu would watch and interpret the actions as best as she could while we looked on. Ammumma smiled and hugged all of us reserving a special seat for Ratna by her side. We huddled as close as we could, attracted by her radiance as her love enveloped us in its warmth.

Marge was the first to notice the sidelong, furtive glances. *Later, Shruthi and Ratna kept an eye on Velan as well. After the first day, he served us tea and went about his tasks in the house.*

Shruthi disliked the sight of him while Marge began to think of ways to alert Deenanna. There was a telephone in Sagu's uncle's home but not the house we were in. There was nothing else to do but bring the guys to the scene of action. Sagu plucked up the courage to inform her parents about Deenanna and Co. after being chastised albeit mildly by Sagu's parents and Ammumma for not joining the girls at the grand home. Arrangements to board in the room upstairs - the one with the double bed were made. More mattresses were bought out from the attic, dusted thoroughly and placed outside in the hot sun. Water was drawn from the kitchen well and poured into cement containers placed within the rudimentary toilets. These were small rooms with sloping floors that had a shallow sinkhole towards a corner that led to the pipes outside. Washing up and bigger jobs necessitated the use of the only facility built downstairs adjacent to the dining area. This had running water and a small toilet bowl. Ammumma's bedroom on the ground floor had an attached washroom with a toilet bowl that was fixed a few years earlier on account of her arthritic knees. The adjacent room that we crowded into also had a miniscule bath area with a ground level squat toilet and mercifully, a tap with running water.

Sagu's parents chose the adjacent room upstairs with the four-poster bed. The next two days were filled with endless chatter and laughter. Since big brother and team had joined us, we felt reassured and safe. Our anxiousness evaporated. We talked more. Laughed more. And were persuaded to stay for a week instead of the three days. Velan and Sagu's dad went to rebook the tickets. Evenings were spent playing badminton and carom. Sagu's parents would join us for a game of cards. We breezed through the week alternating between trips to the pond and tumbling through the attic that were populated by nesting pigeons. Sagu's brother was a sweet child. He simply joined our pack like a little lamb and followed us everywhere.

I loved the house with its tall rafters and pillars of wood. The heavy front door had brass padlocks and almost all the windows and furniture within the house were made of teakwood and wood from the resident jackfruit tree. The gateway on the road led up to the house after a short drive and birds and farm animals dotted the landscape. The house overlooking the paddy fields that were left fallow on account of labor shortage was for us, our spacious playground. We envied Sagu and thought that handling Velan was too small a price to pay in the face of such grandeur. How wrong we were to have made such an assumption!

Apart from Velan who stayed to keep Ammumma company as well as being the general house help, there were two other women who came in to help with the running of the house. Vellachi attended to the tasks that required attention outside of the house such as, sweeping of the front and backyard, washing of all utensils and clothes, feeding the chickens, milking the cows, cleaning the cowshed and chopping firewood for the next day. The other woman named Prema, cleaned the interior of the house, drew water from the well, helped with the cooking, and served food at the table.

The house was run efficiently with Ammumma in charge. Velan, a distant relative and supposedly from a penniless background, was a school dropout. He was Ammumma's right hand and filled in for any task that required execution. On one occasion when the TV simply refused to stream images, Velan clambered onto the slippery red tiled roof and straightened the antenna to its rightful position. It had been knocked down by the wind, apparently. A silent, slight and dim figure who hardly ever spoke, we learnt to avoid him and focused on our activities with gay abandon.

Raw jackfruit and coconut curry for lunch, sliced, deep-fried jackfruit wedges for tea, and succulent portions of the fruit for dessert heralded the jackfruit season. We ate until our stomachs protested after which we were fed rice gruel and toasted lentil wafers for breakfast and lunch. When we howled at this, out came the fish curries and boiled eggs with steaming hot rice. Sagu's parents and Ammumma were generous hosts. We were left to our own devices during the day. Sagu taught us the art of climbing trees. We became adept little monkeys and spent time spinning our little stories perched on the lofty branches while we learnt to avoid being stung by troops of marching red ants that swarmed the bark in rough patches.

There was just over a day to go and we had done nothing about Velan. What would Deenanna do? Scare him or pester him? So far, the man didn't seem to be the monster that Sagu had made him out to be. Perhaps it was her overactive imagination. She did read a lot. But could we just let it be? The 'what if's' brought us back together…. back to what we had planned this little trip for. A hasty conference with Deenanna was required.

Big brother calmed us down, said he would handle it. His chest was all puffed up with importance. His friends nodded their heads sagely. So, we went back to our frenzied activities…now that the hours were drawing to a close.

Evening was pack up time. Sagu pleaded with Ratna to stay for a few more days. I would return with Marge and the big brother team. Our parents would freak out if we stayed any longer and Sagu knew that. Ratna was different. Back to the hostel was not an enticing option. And once again, off went Sagu's father to rebook Ratna's ticket. She would stay for three days. Not a minute more. Sagu was overjoyed and we were glum. We would leave the next morning. In the meantime, we spied Deenanna brandishing his bruised knuckles. All done. Time to split.

Morning dawned. The open jeep had come an hour earlier. Bags needed to be loaded and Velan was called for. Sagu's brother was sent to fetch him since Velan did not seem to be around. As he scurried away, we stole secret looks at each other. Sagu seemed worried. The big brother team seemed blasé about it. Amidst the perplexed looks exchanged by Sagu's parents and Ammumma, the boys hefted the bags onto the vehicle. Sagu's brother returned with the message that Velan was feeling unwell and that he looked sick. With a shrug, Marge, the big brother team and I clambered onto the jeep. Sagu's father came along to see us off. We waved our goodbyes and moved away.

It was back to reality from now. Our idyllic existence had ended and we had to be back in school in a few days' time. The threat of the Board exams loomed over all. We would then go our separate ways after that. For me, this meet was packed with precious memories. Memories that enchanted and drew out the benign. Raw anguish that robbed a house of its essence came later. Immediately afterwards.

*

The Tempest after the Ruin

(The following is an extract reproduced from the archives of The Reader's Review.*'[11])*

The 1990 Machilipatnam Cyclone was the worst disaster to affect Southern India since the 1977 Andhra Pradesh cyclone. The system was first noted as a depression on May 4, 1990, while it was located over the Bay of Bengal about 600 km to the southeast of Madras, India. During the next day the depression intensified into a cyclonic storm and started to escalate rapidly, becoming **a super cyclonic storm** by the morning of May 8. The cyclone weakened slightly before it made landfall on India about 300 km to the north of Madras in the Andhra Pradesh state as **a very severe cyclonic storm** with winds of 165 km/h. The cyclone had a severe impact on India, with over 967 people reportedly killed. Over 100,000 animals also died in the cyclone with the total cost of damages to crops estimated at over $600 million.

***

Those were the days of furore. Of confusion and desperation. Exams dates were postponed until further notice. Our sense of anxiousness was pronounced. Most homes were destroyed either partially or totally. Battered trees, flying debris, choked drains and blocked roads were a common sight. Public life was stilled. Banks and offices were closed and availability of precious commodities was meager. Those who had reserves of cash at hand, managed to get by. Drinking water was scarce and water from the wells turned undrinkable.

There was a wave of typhoid and dysentery and hospitals and private clinics were choc-a-block with patients. The government hospitals had barred fresh patients from entering the premises and public transport had come to a standstill. The Central Government had announced a relief package for those affected and it took almost ten days for the city to get back to its feet.

Since telephone lines were down and electricity was restored only after a week's time, *we (Marge and Shruthi)* assumed that Ratna had reached her hostel room safely, and Sagu would be home just like everyone. With Deenanna away, Marge had a heavy schedule on her hands. Taking care of an asthmatic, occasionally bedridden mother apart from the extra chores took up almost all of her time.

Shruthi on the other hand, was safely ensconced with her family at her aunt's home as soon as word of the cyclone was heard. There they remained until the situation limped back to near normal.

A flurry of activities preceded the settling down state and it took considerable time and effort for the populace to revert to normalcy. It was now time to get a grip and consult the checklist.

- Marge and family – All right. Safe and sound.
- Shruthi and family – Ditto that. By God's grace.
- Ratna – Called the student quarters. All O.K. Bless the school authorities. Would visit her a.s.a.p.
- Sagu and family were not at home. Not. At. Home.

Just what did that mean? There was no Murugan to do the follow up as he had left for his village. He would be back once the opening date of the school was announced.

Now where the heck were they? They had no known relatives or close friends staying in this godforsaken Oothukudi. Did they hear of the cyclone and go back to Malayapuram then? Marge felt unease settle down in the pit of her stomach.

The girls were forbidden to ride down to Sagu's house or take the public bus, considering the situation. Perhaps they could wait for a week and then call her uncle; Marge's father advised. There was a niggling sense of worry that gnawed underneath though.

The lack of information was troubling and an incessant Marge urged her father to accompany her. She had to know. Sitting astride her father on his massive Bullet, they navigated their way through the littered roads to reach Sagu's house. It was locked. The beautiful garden was ripped apart. Totally demolished. It was a devastating sight. Not a good omen. Marge held on to her father's arm and sobbed. She had to meet Shruthi.

*

The small one-bedroom apartment that Shruthi lived in was on the second floor of the LIC Housing colony. She was perched on a ladder wiping down the blades of the ceiling fan. From her vantage point, she registered the two sober faces and scrambled down hastily. Shruthi's mother walked in somberly, as her hands tugged at the ends of her sari. Marge stood stiff, hands at her side, wordlessly looking at Shruthi who stepped forward and enfolded her in a hug.

"There must be a reason, Margie. Don't panic."

"Perhaps, they changed their plan. Probably because of the cyclone..." her voice dwindled.

Shruthi's mother hesitantly added, "You should check with Ratna. She would know. After all, she stayed a few extra days with Sagu." She cautioned, "Why don't you meet her tomorrow and find out before jumping to conclusions?"

11 a.m. the next morning.

Shruthi and Marge entered Ratna's room. The normally spic and span room looked uncared for. Clothes were hung haphazardly on a plastic clothesline inside the room. The room had a faint odor. Of unwashed clothes, stale food and fear. Ratna looked frail. Sallow. She was sitting on her wireframe bed and listlessly looking out of the only window of her room as they entered. Marge and Shruthi were shocked at the change. Ratna's leg stuck out - the good one. The other was hidden beneath her skirt. Marge noticed a deep crack on the Jaipur foot. It was shod in a sandal and stood leaning, forlornly against a wall.

"I'm sorry, Ratna. We should have come sooner for you, taken care of you. You have not been eating well and look ill as well. Get up girl and come home with us," blurted out Marge. Shruthi nodded and sat next to Ratna as if to comfort her. Ratna sighed and it was then that the shivering began. So terrible was the sight that the friends had to hold her down. Gnawing her teeth, wailing pitifully, Ratna clenched and unclenched her hands and lifted them outwards as though in entreaty.

The friends rushed to get the Warden. Apparently, it was the fever that made her delirious. Marge readily agreed to take Ratna home. It was the right thing to do. Shruthi did not have the space. Marge's mom would definitely want Ratna with them and have her father watch out in case of complications. With all the written permissions hastily arranged, an auto rickshaw was hired to take the girls back home. It was providence and Shruthi's mother that saved Ratna, agreed the girls.

*

As they anxiously waited for Ratna's fever to subside, it was announced that all schools were due to reopen in about two to three days' time. The anxiousness resurfaced. It was a difficult time for the families. Getting back to normalcy plus the recouping was tough enough added to which, Ratna was in a state of situation-induced-depression and had to be supported as well. With the railroads now restored, Deenanna arrived the day before the girls were due to begin school. It was a relief as the constant worry was beginning to affect Marge. Ratna showed signs of recovery. Another day or two, and she would be near normal again.

School day dawned and the two girls eagerly scouted their classes for Sagu's presence but there was no sign of her. The constant enquiries from the concerned teachers and others about Ratna and Sagu not being present had the girls with their backs to the wall. Feeling sick from all the concern displayed for which they had no answer, the girls scooted to the music room, which remained unused most times. The after-school rush prompted the girls to hang out for a bit with Murugan who was equally perplexed by Sagupaapaa's absence. He promised to work on the garden and keep a lookout for the family should they reappear.

Eager to meet Ratna and hear from her, the two girls reached home. Shruthi's parents had already arrived. Watching her propped on a wicker chair by the bedside, the girls flanked by Deenanna, and Marge's parents waited for her to speak. No questions were asked. It was clear that they needed answers and Ratna could not avoid them. There was more and they needed to know. It was time.

*

What Happened After

(Ratna's Account)

Silence descended on the house after the guests departed. Everyone seemed forlorn. The summer heat was intolerable and suddenly, normal pastimes seemed uninviting.

Sagu and Ratna decided to complete a Hindi essay, the one earmarked as their vacation homework. Poring over the dictionary and writing down helpful hints amounted to the compilation of a reasonable amount of material that could be stitched together to complete task#1. Writing seemed dull work and the monotony was relieved by occasional gusts of wind that floated in from the outside. As Sagu jotted down the pointers, Ratna, who was by now gazing out of the latticed balcony remarked,

"No sign of creepy V. Anna must have given him good."

"Hmmm," murmured Sagu. After a while, she looked up to find a pensive Ratna staring down at her. "I feel a bit spooked. Unnerved sort of. Shouldn't we inform someone?"

"Don't think so. They might think I made it all up." There was a slight pause. "You don't think that too, do you?" enquired Sagu with a lift of an eyebrow.

Ratna shrugged and remained silent.

After a pause she said, "Frankly speaking, I'm worried."

A coil of dread started to uncoil itself with vicious dexterity and Sagu felt choked. To counter the unpleasantness, she enquired of Ratna with disarming candor and in all innocence, "How old were you when aunty, meaning your mother passed away?"

Shock engulfed Ratna.

This was taboo topic.

A something, that was never to be discussed. As she gazed thunderstruck at her friend, Sagu continued, unaware that she was thinking out aloud. "Why did she do that? Immolate herself? Was it because of your father?" Slight pause.

"You must have been very young. If I were you, I would have left home but with the foot…" her gaze travelled down to Ratna's sock encased feet. Meeting Ratna's incredulous gaze, Sagu merely looked away while her hand surreptitiously crept to enfold her friend's quivering palm.

Several pensive moments later, Sagu got up and dusted the back of her gingham dress. "Shall we walk?" was her simple query.

A wordless Ratna joined her and they picked their way hand-in-hand through ankle high shrubs that grew wild all over the land. Dark skinned men, shirtless, sweat coursing through their bodies were engrossed in cutting the weeds and hand plowing the soil.

As they turned their faces towards the mellow light of the setting sun, Ratna felt weepy and lost. Dry-eyed, she narrated events to this slip of a girl who had intuitively divined all that she had been through. About all the losses that could not be listed and shrugged away gladly, had her mother been at her side today.

*

"My gait was always weird, although not this pronounced, of course," said Ratna with a self-deprecatory laugh. Sagu's shoulder shook in silence. "I was eight when the accident happened," Ratna turned to look at Sagu. "The four of us and *Amma*[19] were crossing the busy street, hands held together in a file. My youngest sister Shakti was cooing away like a steam engine and I was doing the rumbling wheel part. So, we hardly noticed when the lag in the walk ensued. Such was our focus on our little game.

"Amma and my two elder sisters were already off the kerb and they were pulling at the line, shouting for us to quicken our pace. I vaguely recall the truck hurtling towards us and spending the next few weeks in hospital. My phantom foot hurt all the time and it required several painful surgeries and physiotherapy sessions to relieve the pain. I recall my mother crying. Crying over me, I assumed at the time. My radiant mother had been reduced to a mere shadow of her former self and, I was the one to be blamed for that.

"I flew to the pink city of Jaipur soon afterwards with uncle, my mother's brother to try out my new foot*. All this while, I wondered at the continued absence of my father. I endured debilitative pain while learning to walk and support myself. Those harrowing days of sweat mingled with the smell of blood, of the grazed stump that was displayed and inspected countless number of times, the tightening of the clasps to the point of numbness and the worse part of all, the falling over. The falls were random. They occurred every-where. While walking at home or on the street, climbing steps, getting onto a bus, standing in a queue—they (the falls)had nothing to do with gravity and everything to do with self-esteem. It was only the imprint of Amma in my mind's eye that helped me carry on. All I wanted, was to be the apple of her eye again. I could hear her laugh out aloud. See her dimpled smile. I was hungry for food that was cooked by her, not the *dal-roti-sabzi*[12] that I was having here, day in and day out.

"Our train journey back home remained uneventful. I did not visit the lavatory too often fearing the risk of contamination. Though I was comfortably ensconced in the first-class compartment, my thoughts invariably dwelled on the welcome I would receive, once home. My uncle remained silent and withdrawn often, moody and gazed out the window for hours on end. Tiredness I assumed again, owing to responsibility foisted upon him when my father should have taken over. Sympathy at my condition as well, I thought.

"We alighted at the railway station. I refused the use of the portable wheelchair and scanned the crowds for the familiar faces. As uncle ushered me towards the exit while the coolie ran ahead with our bags, I suddenly felt queer. Perhaps they were all ashamed of me! My despondent enquiry dejected uncle and his sloped shoulders sagged even further. He let out a huge sigh and placed his hand on my head and said, 'No child. It's nothing to do with you. Nothing at all.'

"My home looked nothing like the home we lived in. The house looked dark, bereft of light and lacked radiance. The plants on the outside had withered and seemed lifeless. I glanced questioningly at uncle as he directed the auto rickshaw towards his home, two houses away.

"The colorless welcome that I received and the outpouring of emotions that had thence been walled in burst open like a flood. All the memories of familial bonding, gaiety and fun were to remain memories henceforth. Amma was gone. Twin tragedies in quick succession had dulled her to the point of apathy. Not being able to deal with the pain had magnified her sense of hopelessness threefold. Having to cope with the loss of her child's mobility added to the shock of knowing that her husband had cheated on her, that too, after several years of marriage, dispelled the inherent radiance. Adding fuel to the fire was on learning that the 'other woman' was pregnant, forcing her to take the extreme step. My mother's stature in society, her respectability, had been cruelly destroyed. The infidelity and the gossip mongering had been the hardest to bear. For a fraction of a second, my mother became a woman. She thought only for herself, about herself. By the time the mother in her realized the colossal leap that had been taken, destiny had played her hand.

"What was the loss of a foot when compared to the loss of one's mother? When a giant vacuum sucks out everything that is within you, all that is left is the emptiness. An empty room, strangers, a new school; these remained meaningless until fate brought you to me." Sagu tightened her grip for a millisecond, the action indicative of her emotion.

"All those thoughts, the deliberate suppression, you unlocked with a single statement. Was I so easy to read?" The two smiled at each other. The sun had set and a slight chill had dampened the air. Shivering slightly, they hastened back to the house, the mounds of freshly turned earth slowing their efforts.

***

** A short note on the famed Jaipur foot:*

It is in the city Jaipur, Rajasthan; that a nonprofit organization dedicated to fitting the disabled with artificial limbs was established. Scores of patients gather from across the country as well as neighboring countries in the center's front yard and by the end of the day, more than 35 persons would make the long journey back to their homes and communities outfitted with a new prosthetic leg that promised them a more active and functional future. The entire treatment is absolutely free of cost. Although the Jaipur foot has been around for over five decades, it is an irony that till date, it remains the most used and well-loved prosthetic in many parts of the world and continues to make a huge difference in the lives of the disadvantaged.

The modern Jaipur foot uses two blocks of microcellular rubber and an ankle section made of lightweight willow wood; the foot also uses nylon cords, which are embedded in the rubber. Additional rubber is used to cover these units and to provide the final form of a human foot, accounting for flexibility and shock absorption. These two sections, along with the Jaipur foot and a cuff suspension, complete the prosthesis for dynamic alignment. The external cover uses a cosmetic rubber cushion compound, which gives the prosthetic the color and texture of natural skin. This unit is several times stronger than a normal human leg and provides mobility that is close to the natural movement of patients.

***

The evening flew past and dinner was a glum affair. After the previous day's hullabaloo, small talk was noticeably absent. It was suggested that the two girls sleep in Ammumma's room, on the twin bed. Mournful acqueisance followed the quiet night.

There was no sign of Velan the whole of next day as well. A rising disquiet continued to disturb the girls. Ammumma could be seen motioning with regard to his lack of empathy while the rest of the household went about their tasks. Ratna's query of the previous evening began to surface and take root in Sagu's thoughts. Thoughts turned into little demons. Her face flamed and sweat coursed down the sides in tiny rivulets.

"Was it all a mistake?" she thought.

"Those dark looks. The unwanted caress." Did she translate them into something uninhibited and fiery?

And, Deenanna's retribution… Did she instigate violence against an innocent man?

All that she knew were derived from books. Was theory different from the real?

The girls spent their entire time outdoors, forlorn, hoping against hope that they had not made a cruel mistake.

Conveying an apology crossed their minds but the two felt awkward about meeting Velan. Ratna was secretly glad that she was leaving the day after. After an evening excursion to the temple presided by the family deity, dusk fell and soon, it was time to be in bed. The girls pleaded to be allowed to sleep in the room that contained the twin beds. Sagu wailed and begged her Ammumma to let them be. The girls were allowed after a short pause and off they went upstairs triumphantly. The door was bolted from inside as per instructions and the girls listened to songs that soothed on their leather encased Philips transistor radio.

"Sagooo, Sagooo," floated Sagu's mother's voice from below. The radio was switched off and the door unbolted. "Ennamma? What is it?" enquired Sagu.

"Are you both fine? You have not taken the bottled water. Do you want me to bring it up?"

"We are good, Amma. Go back to sleep."

The two girls settle down and were soon fast asleep.

But the door—

Girl, Do. Not. Forget. The. Door.

*

Ratna sniffed and looked down at the floor. A pregnant pause ensued that reeked of doom.

The group around her was hushed… huddled together. Knowing what was to come. Dreading it. Helpless.

It was as though one among them was soon to be ripped apart. Mercilessly torn into pieces.

Marge's mother sighed. Drew in an audible breath. Shuddering gasps ensued. Marge held her tight.

"She was the only one who knew." Ratna gazed at Shruthi who looked away. Tears rolled down her face. "The only one who guessed how my mother quit." She continued, "Amma left my three sisters and me with a father who was a cheat." It was sometime during this dark phase that the insurance papers with regard to the accident was sorted out and with the interest paid out as monthly remittance, Ratna chose to further her studies away from her guardian. The man she called her father.

Student quarters, she chose over family.
Until, we came along.
Until, Sagu lent her her heart.

*

He came that night. The door was unlatched and we slept on. The door was locked once again. But it was not Sagu's hand that did it.

A hand clamped over a mouth, cutting off screams. Reason struggled to rise. It was dark and groping hands flailed. There was a dull thump… of the foot falling onto its side. A wild struggle ensued, accompanied by the rustle of clothes and hot breathing.

"Ratna?" Sagu's tentative call rang out. Silence. Stillness. A hand reached out for the foot. Palm clutched cold air. So she reached down, grabbed the foot and swung it in the direction of the shirtless body. There was a stifled groan and a dull thump. Ratna had managed to slide off from below Velan onto the floor and crawl towards the door. Sagu hefted the foot once again as Velan prepared to grab Ratna.

In the darkness, Sagu noticed the dishevelment. "No," she whispered. "Not her." The murderous glint in Velan's eyes dimmed and he paused for a second.

"Please don't," went the painful entreaty.

As his hand inched forward, the foot came down once again. But this time, he was ready. Avoiding the move, he lunged towards Sagu and the foot rolled towards the wall.

The sound of a hard slap resounded within the small room. The air remained motionless. Sagu's head rolled and pounded. Throbbing lips that were split wide open struggled to form words.

Steel bands imprisoned her, prompting the whimper. "Go Ratna, just go."

*

And the terrified Ratna fled. Releasing the bolt, she hopped towards the wooden stairwell. Stomach heaving. Hopping. Gasping. Reaching out for the handhold. Gripping with slippery fingers. Pausing to listen to the wild struggle behind her.

She barely felt the steps, the eight wooden ones she had rolled over. It was quick, guaranteed to break her neck or, her one good leg. But Ratna was safe.

For a second, she felt herself meander and her eyes closed. Ears ringing, head throbbing, she forced herself to stir.

There was a flurry of movement. Lights were switched on.

And that was how the elders found her, crumpled and bent. Limbs askew, nightdress in tatters, keening softly on the landing. As they struggled to comprehend the fright in her eyes, their looks involuntarily turned, to seek out her beloved companion. For the explanation that was required.

As the pitiful shrieks and rhythmic whumps filtered through the still night, Sagu's parents remained rooted to the spot unable to understand.

It was simultaneous. The realization and fading away of the intrusive sounds into the sensation of dread, that slowly crept in. Sagu, beautiful child, how could this happen? Light of our lives, how could the blight wipe away the glare?

*

From the Bend to the Turning Point –

Kurinji

Sitting under the shade of a tall coconut palm, watching the green waters flowing past, inner thoughts quite often spoken aloud, my queer behavior became my cloak. It helped reduce visibility. Passers-by avoided looking at me. Out of deference for my poor mother I suppose. To them, I was like Kurinji. Another hapless soul. Another lost one. I couldn't care less though. My fears, angst, gender were all proving to be an impediment. What more could bash me up?

I wondered about Kurinji though. From my mother, I gathered that she was a drifter. Perhaps she had a sad story to tell. But no one listened. She was thought of as mute. And so she set up base, by the communal well. Beneath the large frangipani tree that covered the place with its fragrant blossoms. The women obsessed over her. Speculation was rife that she was not quite alright. And so she was christened Kurinji - after the blooms that were rarely seen but noted for their beauty. And the name seemed to please her given her love for the champakam flower. When she was called, her response would often be a pre-occupied half-smile.

Once, I had peeked at her from a distance and found her gazing at me. Was she as curious about me as I was of her? Abashed, I had run away and taken my place here. Everything about the beckoning had been gentle. The half shade, the salty warm air that flowed over my body, everything had offered comfort. Perhaps Kurinji had listened to the snide remarks being passed about me and smiled that familiar half-smile of hers. We were both lost souls I think. Similar in nature. Silent, absorbed, and withdrawn from the prying eyes and lips.

I had never sought to intrude and neither did she make any attempt to invade my space. It was as if our borders were pre-defined. I could soon be christened with a name that the community thought fit and the thought displeased me. Suddenly, just suddenly, I wanted to move on. Continue with my search elsewhere. My mother would accompany me in meek suppliance I suppose.

Were my days of solitude reaching an inevitable end? Perhaps nature was forcing her hand. Destiny and Nature - two words that could be compared, yet, seemed radically different. I have always felt that both entities are the same. We are all part of the same rat race. A cycle that is unending. Individual differences and experiences are what make us unique.

Ratna was an unnecessary spoke in the wheel that terrible day. The one that was not meant to be. When a cat stalks its prey, its silent watch initially serves to deflect the opponent. The watch though, never wavers. The deception doesn't lessen. The initial slip from the pursuit creates a lull but the patient wait of the tail with the twitch never falters.

The bashing that Velan received from the three youths only served to enrage him further. What seemed to be an untouchable commodity served to entice even further... a fact that was highlighted by the undue aches and pains on account of the ferocious assault. Just as a bully targets the weak, Ratna seemed easily accessible. Availability of yet another prey accentuated the sense of arousal. Lust, anger and patience coupled with carelessness gave the opportunity Velan required that fateful night.

My reverie was interrupted by shouts and loud talk. People were seen moving hurriedly towards the direction of the frangipani tree. *What could be the matter*, I wondered. Joining the melee as I got caught between bodies swaying and crushed together, I caught the general drift of the conversation. Someone by then had noticed the odd girl (me) in their midst. Hands turned me back. Prodded me on towards my temporary place of stay.

I tried to resist. An inherent dread had turned my insides to jelly. My legs turned to stone and I refused to budge from where I stood. People exclaimed at my odd behavior. In the end, a neighbor was asked to take me home. In their eyes, I was young and shouldn't be privy to the scene that lay just a few yards away.

The neighbor related the unfortunate incident to my mother in great detail. It was Kurinji. She had been violently violated. Her remains were being taken to the electric crematorium. How could anyone be callous enough to disturb the peace of a helpless, harmless being was beyond comprehension. The neighbor tut-tutted her sympathy for the poor soul. Kurinji was vague, kept to herself and was known to be 'not right in the head.' If there were no hope for an abstract being, how safe would normal women in the general vicinity be?

My mother was advised to refrain from letting her child wander outdoors, all by herself. After all, if Kurinji was harmed, then perhaps I could possibly be the next target.

*

So, we bundled up all over again. Gathered together our meager possessions. It was time to escape yet another hellhole.

And I agreed with that. For a heart-stopping moment, mother and child bonded over a gaze.

Rustle. Pack. Time to join the family. Memories were not to resurface. They were to be stored away, far from all necessities that conform to the normal.

Mother's mumblings helped me box them up. Block their vitality thus help them lose their relevance. I watched her carry forth. Rush to the neighbor to request for two train tickets to be booked for the night and hurry away from the non-essentials. Only that mattered now.

The room seemed to have a sense of the oppressed.

Refuge turned oppressor.

The preference was hence, to wait for several hours on the railway platform hoping that the train arrived on time. The waiting seemed interminable.

Our inspection of the tea stall, book shop, mobile snack sellers, people and packed vehicles waiting to get to their destination calmed our burning hearts.

"It was meant to be her. That was part of the plan." My hesitant statement brought about a curious stillness to mother's body.

"I couldn't let that happen, amma. She had gone through enough." Gulps turned to sobs.

"I needed to protect her. I tried my best. It just didn't turn out well," I began to sob in earnest. I felt gutted, raw. Aching interminably from the loss. Loss of girlish innocence. The loss of something far, far precious. My grief knew no bounds. I tried to curl up on my mother's lap. Her tears fell on my hands as she drew me closer, to her bosom.

"I'm sorry for not confiding in you. I just thought it would fly away, disappear like in the stories," I said through pain-laced hiccups.

"Shh, my child. You were never at fault. It was us, never you. We failed you, child. Failed miserably."

And just after that, came the clamor of the train accompanied by the assorted hustle. The journey back home seemed calm, almost placid. We were spent, drained. Our eyes and hearts were blank and tearless.

It was then that I knew that a choice had to be made. Kurinji - my motivator, it was decision time.

Goal #1: complete High school.
Goal #2: Med school.

I now understood where I would be needed the most.

*

A Constant Refrain

I was all at sea, Kurinji, my apologies.
While I wallowed in misery, you turned nemesis.
Jolted me from the apathy.
Apologies, for I did not try acquaint
Self-absorbed, a poor excuse
The hand that forced was yours, I know.
A wake up call from despondent slumber,
To negate the rush of anger at the feel of helplessness,
Incoherent rage at a move so foul.
Undecided has turned decisive.
To achieve, despite failings
There are more,
More who require the gentle hand.
The rise after the burning, that is to be contended with.
It is time to gather, quell the fever
Make the plunge with the tide.
And, move in with the swell.

*

MAY 1999

The routine went this way every time. My sing-a-long helped relieve the boredom. What could a bank or any conglomerate offer a fresh grad cum inexperienced bumpkin without a shard of experience and a dime to her name? Nothing.

*Only a **nothing**, colored with the whiff of sarcasm.*
*The **nothing**, that is delivered without a tinge of regret.*
__Nothing__ as always - except for the shallow curl of that upper lip.

Bah!
Block it. Box it. Sagu, this too shall pass.

In the end, Sagu's father gave away a parcel of ancestral land that was bequeathed to him to purchase a plot of land in the town. The seeds were sown.

The building blocks for the Sagarika Charitable Hospital were laid. Back then (year 2000), it was known as the Sagarika General clinic. The trust was formed after the expansions. That was Manu's suggestion. Chandrashekhar would take care of the daily operations. The boy, my brother's son, grew up in our household and was quite attached to me as I was to him.

My child. In place of the one I'll never have. A decision I have never regretted. And one that Manu supported. Manu breezed into my life just when I needed the balance. He chose to be my respite.

Admin Head, essence of my world.

I was secure. And so was he.

*

Before the Wave

The time spent in the consultation room waiting for patients during the first few months certainly gave us several anxious moments. Never had time stretched out so fine, so evenly distanced out that it felt like being on a watch for a debilitative disease that made its gradual progression in stop-motion time lag sequence.

Father took up the post of the receptionist-cum-cashier. His natural exuberance was quickly staunched chiefly due to the fact that there were no calls and neither was the cash flowing in. For the most part, listlessness and the heat had induced a dull stupor in all of us. Murugan hobbled outside digging and watering the straggly assortment of plants he was trying to coax life into.

I developed a penchant for swatting flies using a rolled up newspaper. The accuracy improved when the angle of delivery was sufficiently tilted, I discovered. My mother gifted me a plastic fly swatter after watching my concerted efforts. I could sense her exasperation. In those days, marketing one's capabilities meant having a travelling artist proclaim all of your valiant and heroic contributions in the field of medicine through a loudspeaker perched on a tricycle. Such a practice was abhorrent to my family. We had 'middle class' scruples. That did not include extreme measures such as these in the pursuit of recognition. You were in a saintly profession. Your status was soon to be elevated to the haloed position that almighty mortals existed in. The torturous wait was hence, to continue.

We spent hours chatting. My parents and I. Tried to make up for the time that was lost. I spoke to them about the Zenana. About Shruthi and Marge. The happy times that were contrived and paced through with reckless abandon. Of Marge's constant fights with her brother to attempt master their father's Bullet. Deenanna was the original MCP. He believed in the adage that girls ought to live and die in the kitchen, apart from conducting the necessary reproductory and household-based tasks. It made our blood boil to hear her talk about anna's restrictions when her parents seemed to be relatively easy-going. However, when we needed a knight-in-shining-armor or, a shield as cover, he would readily come over, eager to prove his might.

Shruthi was already proving her worth, with her culinary skills being honed in part by her paatti—veritable grandmother, who was a treasure trove of recipes that were a family heirloom. The girl didn't require a degree in home science for heaven's sake! Her lemon and tamarind rice, tiny round dosas with coconut chutney and, fried lentil cakes made us double over in delight. She would always bring along an additional box as takeaway since we were extremely receptive to her burgeoning talent. The student quarters served up awful dishes anyway and Ratna required the extra nourishment as well. By the time she was out of school, Shruthi would be able to man several households effortlessly I opined, to my parent's mirth.

As for Ratna, the girl was thinner than a drumstick who pecked through her food like a sparrow. She had her reasons to continue her focus on education, we knew. But was a total patch-out when compared to Shruthi. Show her a knife and a peeler, and you would know. We did not want to end up with a missing arm or leg so we let her be for the most part.

As for the heaven that was her point of origin, ah, that was another matter altogether. Ootacamund comes uppermost to my mind these days. Those rivulets, the terraced farms on which 'English' vegetables were grown; carrots, potatoes, cauliflowers and long beans, grown by the Badagas, the native tribe and original farmers of the land. Onward and deep into the recesses of the terraced steps we would walk through, watching the elderly Todas in their miniscule mud huts. The name, Ootacamund was shortened to Ooty by the Englishmen who found the cool weather of the hills amenable during the hot months between May-July in Madras only to gradually embrace it as their summer retreat.

Ratna's uncle took us on a jeep ride to their ancestral home deep down the hills. The road wound through making me sick and I was good naturedly mocked at for my weak stomach. Her family was a respectable one I gathered as there were many who stopped and waved at us as we passed them by. The house was crumbly but grand, fashioned out of wood, mud, and thatch. There were tiny windows that were boarded from the inside. This was where the ancestors lived, I was informed. The house was not being razed to preserve what was left of the olden ways. The interior was gloomy and I wondered at the presence of humans within this framework that had an absolute lack of daylight. Coming out of the dingy interior to face the weak sunshine made me feel dizzy once again and I remember being offered a glass of water by a kind lady. The smell of the eucalyptus in the air revived me and we were soon on our way back. Uncle had done some basic checks and seemed to be satisfied that the house was still holding itself together.

I suddenly wished to be back at Sujata akka's home, walk around to the backyard and stop at the fence overlooking the slope that was slightly steep and covered with ferns, grasses and wildflowers. The slope bottom was strewn with small rocks and fallen eucalyptus leaves. We would slide down the slope laughing and tumbling, our *kurtis*[7] bunched around our waists with bits of leaves and mud sticking to us as we reached the fragrant but spiky bottom. Our bodies had the pleasant scent of the eucalyptus and crushed fern leaves as we scrambled our way back to the top to start the slide all over again. Ratna turned out to be a mad hatter. It was as though, with me around, she threw caution to the winds. Her air of severity disappeared and she learned to undo the shackles that had been readily adorned. We became careless, lazy and habitually happy. Free of encumbrances, we learned to be wholesome again. The trip had given me a temporary lease of life and I felt invigorated. Ooty was a magical place and I hoped that the charm still lingered.

*

Since the clinic and the land belonged to my father, the issue of rent payment was one worry off our list. The home fires were feeble though reduced to the kindling stage. We had not reached desperate levels as yet.

My books were put up inside a lone glass-fronted bookcase. Proud and shining in their new covers, I dusted them once in a while and admired my precious collection. Enthusiasm levels, however, dipped soon after and feeble efforts at a later stage to continue with the said practice had been abandoned. Mustering one's energy for something significant was fine. Something as exciting as the hopscotch games played during childhood. It was not to be wasted for something as trivial as dusting of books, however valuable they were deemed to be.

Now for the hopscotch games that turned us into the fiercest of warriors. How we hopped away on the sand! Cousins engaged in mock fights, shrill voices and all. Battle lines were blurry, drawn with fingertips that were thin and stumpy on shifting sand. I remembered the fingers sheathed in vivacity.

Once the game paced on, the level of fierceness increased. It became a race; a race to be finished… a race that had to be won. When I sensed defeat, I often fell. Faked the fall. I had mastered the art of hitting the sand after a pre-calculated jump.

I remembered the sand in the mouth. The nose snorts that burnt through and bought a fierce round of hacking coughs and tearing up of the eyes. The blurry lines would be grudgingly cleared and a fresh round would be declared the next day. But boy, the fall and the subsequent discomfort were worth the sacrifice.

Memories of the taste of the sand, acid-sour, bitter and gritty laced with saliva rose up. There had to be a way. I needed another Kurinji to jog me out of the current rut. God forgive me, but what was to be done?

*

The Beginning of the Avalanche

Days flew by. Broad hints were passed. Money was scarce. Even Murugan's loyalty was beginning to be put to the test. A neighboring conglomerate had offered a good price for the plot of land on which stood the clinic. There was no value for achievers who had decided to dedicate their lives for the betterment of society. Snide remarks by outsiders about income spent towards higher education that later entailed in swatting of flies and rehashing of dreams were made day in and out.

Where was this 'so-called' exalted position in society that an aspiring doctor was to occupy, lamented my mother. "Koteeswari - I hate the word! An illiterate god-man for one, would have had a hundred thousand minions waiting to offer blind obeisance," she harangued in anger.

"Do observe the mindset of the common folk. Money down the drain for such vagaries, but justified nevertheless. A few rupees towards consultation that too discounted, by the doctor with-the-golden-hand, and everyone turns up their noses," her tirade continued.

A mother's love for her own could turn reverence for the Holiest of the Holy into dispassion should circumstances color events, I realized. This was especially true if her progeny was being unfairly targeted for no reason other than the unknown entity named fate, forcing one's hand. Suppressing my amusement, I nodded in agreement.

It was then… suddenly, that something stirred. And, churned. Thinking of the wait in a long queue under the blazing sun. That throng.
The lemon. Snug within my palm.
The twinkling eyes, mischievous smile.
The Wise One beckoned.

Murugan was quickly dispatched to the studio to get two framed 16.5 X 11.7 inches pictures within the shortest time frame possible. He was to personally hand over the items to me.

It was late evening when he arrived. One of the images was hung adjacent to the name board outside the clinic and the other, within my room. On the wall, high up and facing the patients. Decorated with a single garland of fresh roses and the familiar face wreathed in that mischievous smile!

The trickle started followed by the throng. Queues that were a mile long necessitated the handout of numbered coupons. The doctor that was blessed by the Wise One was here, in their midst. None had known until the picture was put up.

Everything and everyone was now looked upon with reverence. The doctor, her father, the stethoscope, her writing pad, the consultation room, the bookcase with the books, just about the entire structure with its occupants seemed to take on an extra halo that symbolized benevolent grace. The clinic by itself turned into an iconic landmark of the area. Men, women, and children sometimes, cattle came to visit the lady who was blessed by the One while she was still a girl.

When enquired by curious members of the throng as to whether she was the favored one, a slight smile would grace her features and thus satisfy the seekers. Father favored this mode of reply as well. It seemed to work.

And the mischievous smile graced the premise for a few more years. Until, experience took the upper hand. For the renowned, introductions weren't a necessity. The contribution of the Wise One helped spear the drum roll. The photo on the wall lost its significance after a period of time.

*

Core Z's gotten a whiff. Whiff of what's brewing. What cannot be undone now would be the news spreading across group members. Thanks to instant messaging, everyone would know for sure.

Ah well, there's only one sane thing Sagarika's got to do. Check into the palliative care unit. Manu wouldn't approve of care at home. Too many memories lasted there anyway. The unit was our last dream project completed as a group. Surrounded by my core (handpicked) team and all the others, I'm sure I could manage. After all, what better way to check on the system than by being a part of it?

I could fill in the feedback form with suggestions for improvement and areas that needed more work. After all, the charitable concern needs to take care of the people who need love and care the most. Especially the ones without families. Here, we would be their rock, their mainstay. Making it easier for them to let go - leave with a sense of relief and without painful emotions dwelling within their hearts.

I want to get that feel. And know that what I set out to do, I did right. Chandru will take care of the rest.

Manu… my Manu is waiting to hold my hands. I need to ride an absurdly heavy Atlas bicycle again. Feel the breeze fan my face, laugh so hard that my stomach jiggles. Fall over and get up, smiling at the pain.

- Marge – soul twin,
- Shruthi – our Buddha with the punch, and,
- Ratnalakshmi K.B. – of the space within my heart…, this vulnerable goof wants the Zenana all over again. What's life without a few arguments anyway?

I smile in anticipation and wait for them to arrive.

And what of Velan, you might wonder.
In life, learning experiences comes with a price.
I consider that chapter to be a valuable lesson learnt.
I was blessed with so much more.
It was just a lesson. Only that.

*

PART II

Murugan

(Reminiscences)

(As translated from Thamizh to English)

The village I belong to –Gramayur is twenty-five kilometers away from Oothukudi. I was a small time farmer and worked diligently on my small plot of land. Plants that flowered were what I focused upon. Fragrant jasmine during the summer and orange kanagambaram also called firecracker flowers, during the cooler season. The entire stretch of land was used for the cultivation of flowers and so I had a thorough working knowledge of most of the flowering species of the native kind and, all the necessities required for increasing productivity. The soil was deemed most suitable for this purpose since generations.

Most of the farmers had their plots handed down by their fathers and almost all had availed of loans from the richest man of the town, the *Zamindar*[14]. Thus the entire harvest from the lands went directly to the *Pannayar*[15] who deducted payment from the interest accrued on the principal amount.

The vicious cycle ensured that most farmers struggled under mounds of debt. Other unfortunate members had their lands forcibly taken away as their forefathers had already mortgaged the plots for paltry sums to get their families going.

Rather than succumbing to misery and ending of lives as was the only solution most farmers and their families resorted to, I left home in search of a way to sustain my hunger-wracked family. Lacking an education, penniless and severely undernourished, I begged and hiked my way from *Gramayur*[12] to the town of Oothukudi.

Landing the job of watchman at the Silver Flower Higher Secondary School was to me, the Goddess-sent safety net. It was the year 1986 and being paid a minimal amount of 250 rupees, kept my family afloat for quite some time.

It was around this time that the antics of the four friends caught my attention. Having the wife and two children back in the village, I quickly developed an affection for the girls, most notably for my '*Sagu paapaa*'[9]. She was my little one.

Lively conversations between us soon led to a deep friendship resulting in several visits to her home after which, I took over the task of bringing into life their garden, which soon blossomed. Under my direction, a tiny vegetable garden at the back was also developed. Additionally, Sagu began to train me in Spoken English. Rudimentary phrases such as, "Good morning Sir/Madam. How are you?" or, "Sir/Madam is not in office. Could you please come again?" on behalf of an extremely busy staff member ensured my popularity among the management personnel. The effect of the usage of these standard phrases in situations that called for a specific response resulted in ludicrous situations at times. For example, when a parent approached me for directions towards the washroom, the reply, "Madam is not in office. Could you please come again?" would confound them. After several futile attempts at gaining a grip on the language, I gave up. I detested being laughed at. The local language that I spoke fluently was sufficient enough to convey what needed to be conveyed.

It was after the fourth summer that the cyclone hit the coast of Tamil Nadu. Fearing for my family's safety, I hastened to Gramayur and was hence unaware of the situation that had toppled Sagu paapaa's small world.

Upon my return and after several visitations to her home with my anxiousness on the rise, I made the decision to visit Malayapuram by bus and discover what became of the family. Something akin to dread kept tugging at my insides as I prayed to Goddess *Maariyamman*[17] to protect the one I cared most about, throughout the journey. On getting down at the main terminal, I made general enquiries at the local phone booth-cum-tea shop, refreshed myself at the pay-and-use washroom and then climbed into a jeepney that was packed with travelers. It was apparent that the Malayapuram house and its inhabitants were well known and directions to reach there were immediately supplied by the locals. It was clear from their demeanor that nothing was amiss and I felt relieved.

The walk from the main road to the house was pleasant and I admired the greenery and lush foliage that dotted the wayside. I reached the massive gates and was struck at the grandeur of the sight. Here was a house that was majestic and towering. It stood slightly elevated and was surrounded by luxuriant fruit bearing trees. Massive bougainvilleas lined the driveway interspersed with hibiscus shrubs that bloomed in profusion. Also to be seen were my favorite, the jasmine growing wildly next to the roses. A tulsi (basil) plant stood on a mounted platform in the front yard right before the steps leading to the carved wooden door.

As I approached the entrance, I became aware of a peculiar stillness. The sound of a dog barking from someplace close could be heard. I went up the steps and rang the doorbell waiting to see a familiar face smile and run towards me. After several minutes, the house help, Prema, unbolted the door. The grave face inspected me for a few seconds and indicated that I was to wait.

My first view of Sagupaapaa's Ammumma was not a pleasing one. Ammumma looked frail and weak. She was supported by the house help and stumbled towards the nearest chair. Her gray hair stood up in wisps all around her face and she directed her gaze at me. Understanding who I was and the purpose of my visit, Ammumma broke down. Prema had also gathered into a heap and crouched by her feet in distress.

From Prema, I gradually pieced together the gruesome incident that had befallen the family. I wailed and cried for the little one. "Where was the perpetrator? The one who does not deserve to live?" I angrily demanded. I wanted to strangle him with my bare hands. Such was my rage at the cruelty he had meted out to an unsuspecting, innocent soul. I couldn't bear the thought of Sagu paapaa being hurt. I had never seen her breakdown or cry at the slightest incident. Her impish grin would be wiped away now and a black wave engulfed my heart. As I continued to question Prema, I was informed that his body was found floating in the unused pond the very next day. What had happened to him, how he met his end, no one knew. None at the house cared either. But Sagu and her family had left, leaving Ammumma all alone. Their whereabouts were unknown and Ammumma was slowly sinking, succumbing to her grief.

And so, I left the house that I had just admired. All I wanted was to reach the school. Agony and despair assailed my soul. I had reached the end of my search. The three girls and their families had to be told. I would wait. Wait for Sagupaapaa's call. She would call. My heart said that she would. Of that I was sure.

*

It was in the year 2000 that I got the call I had been waiting for. Ten long years was the length of the wait. I was weeding the vegetable patch after school dispersal when the postman hand-delivered the postcard. There was a single line written in Thamizh on it with an address. I packed my bags the very next day and bid adieu to the school after informing all the Sirs and Madams I had known throughout my time in school, of my decision. There was no hesitation or qualms at letting go of the only job I had ever known.

My Sagu paapaa needed me. The little one wanted to see me.

*

The initial year was an exacting one. The family's financial capabilities had been stretched to the limit. *Periya aiyya*[16], Sagu paapaa's father, was penniless, having sold all his possessions that included his ancestral land, to build the clinic for his daughter on the *Ravirajapuram*[12] plot. But the locals knew that the young Doctor was inexperienced. Under a misguided understanding that the family was extremely well off, criticisms abounded and personal visits were hence hardly made or encouraged. The family's ostracization was complete.

I was not expected to lend my hand for long but the family had not understood me well. My love for them preceded any sense of obligation or gratitude. I had prayed to Amma Maariyamman to bring back paapaa to my life, so that I could make amends. My Goddess was watching. She would set things right. My little one would be the one to watch out for. Litanies of her achievement would spread far and wide. I would not move from this place until I watched that happen with my own eyes.

Penury leads to desperation. I had seen it ages ago, in Gramayur. We were at the brink of it again. We subsisted on rice gruel and the few scraps that I managed to coax out of the lifeless earth. Each day that passed seemed more harrowing than the previous one.

One night I dreamt that Maariyamman was smiling at me. Smiling at Sagu paapaa as well. It was sometime in the afternoon the next day that Amma's loud lamentations seemed to startle *Saguma*[10] and then stupefy her for a while. As I cycled to the studio to get a postcard-sized picture enlarged, I was left wondering at the change in her behavior. We hung the pictures as per her direction and settled for the night.

The next day brought in the tremendous change that I had prayed for. My Maariyamman; my Devi had signaled in the avalanche. We were going to be on our toes forever! My Sagupaapaa was now Dr. S. How regal that sounded! I would be a witness to the change that was coming. It made me feel very proud and satisfied.

*

It was in the year 2006, during the monsoon period that *Manaiyya*[16] was brought to us. His professional details had reached *Periyaaiyya*[16] and a meeting was arranged. Manaiyya was running an organization up in the north and seemed to be a very important person. I learnt from Saguma that he was also her childhood friend. From personal experience, Manaiyya seemed to be a humble man. Very down to earth and simple at heart.

The expansion of the clinic to the hospital that you are seeing today is solely due to the pioneering vision and dedication of Manaiyya and his team. *Doctoramma*[16] (Saguma) and Manaiyya were quite close. I have noted this about her, that unnerving instinct. The people that she chose to have around her, stayed loyal that was of the unswerving kind.

Look at her childhood friends. Look at me. To this day, we look up to her. She's blessed. That is what it is.

I remained associated with the organization up until 2015. My wife has been long gone. I feel the pain in my bones now. Old age I think. Although I still continue to supervise the gardeners and the workers here, it's time for me to shift to Gramayur and stay with my children and their families. They are well settled now. Thanks to Manaiyya, who has taken good care of them, all I require for now is to spend the rest of my days with my grandchildren and have my ashes scattered near the vicinity of the temple of Goddess Maariyamman.

*

It is June 2017 and I'm back in the room I'd lived in for over fourteen years. I've heard the news and, it's not good. Wild horses won't drag me away from here this time and if this one time I need to defeat that something which is darker, the one that spells the end of everything, I would do that gladly. Give up my soul in exchange for a life more precious.

Manaiyya's leaving has left Saguma heartbroken, I know, but that does not signify the end of everything. Her next bout with greatness ought to begin. I have seen it happen before and just this once, before I go, I wish for it to happen again. Crawling on all fours, if I could help it. For that, Maathae (Divine mother), I need to see you smile at my Saguma once again. Consider it my last wish.

*

Manavlal Yadav

I was born with the name Manavlal Yadav. That I would be called Manaiyya one day was an inconceivable thought. I rather fancied names like Ray or, Allen. Manavlal Yadav or, Manu was way better than Manaiyya though.

Well, well, what's in a name, Mr. Fancy Pants, I heard her enquire with a hint of laughter. Dim echoes of that honey-dipped voice lilting, rising and, dipping as the occasion warranted. Sometimes, with a trace of sarcasm that dripped and stained while at others, the firm with a hint of compassion shone through. I had never known that the tone and tenor of a voice by itself could be this mesmerizing. Like tongues snaking out, feeling, caressing and the gradual, slow submersion into its depths.

When the letter of enquiry came from Ms Sagarika General Hospital, I recognized the feeling. The sudden churn. That name. A most unusual one - Sagariga, I had called her then. Sa, Ri, Ga, the first three notes of the sapthaswaras-the basic seven notes that form the foundation of classical music; any music. Its western counterpart began as Do, Re, Mi, and, ended in Do. I remembered the rendition of Julie Andrews in the 'Sound of Music'. Of all the children watching the film, with rapture on their faces. Munching through handfuls of dry roasted peanuts, and non-crisp popcorn, school water bottles hanging from our necks, with bare feet or school sock encased feet that were snug within sandals. Sagarika was engrossed and hummed along gazing intently at the screen. Our grasp of the language was limited and we tried to follow the lives of the Von Trapp family chiefly through the visual imagery and the wondrous songs. Such was its impact that we imagined ourselves to be the Von Trapp children marching away and allowing Sagarika to take the place of Julie chiefly because she could sing. And she had a voice! There was no doubt about that.

Many joyful hours we had spent after school in the hot sun, tramping behind her, imagining ourselves to be flying about and living our lives in a castle. Sagarika's obsession with the songs gave me the chance to rechristen her as Doremi. Not that she liked Sagarika anyway. The memory bought a smile to my lips.

Obnoxious brat she was; defiant, with a devil-may-care attitude. That fistfight with her a few days before she left was epic. She just wouldn't give up. And that was all we had talked about for days after they had left.

She had given me good. Matched a punch for every punch that I handed out. Kick for a kick and, slap for all those slaps.

In the end, I was exhausted but determined to win. Inevitably, that led to a hollow feeling. Of having hurt her. I got roasted at home for bashing a girl. However fiery she was, Doremi was a fighter. Being the only girl among my gang of boys who were stout locals, the respect she had earned was grudging and soon turned to admiration.

I flipped the folded letter open and studied the address printed below. No. 143, Malcolm Road, Ravirajapuram, Chennai. So that's where they had gone. From the northeast to the south of India. I wondered how they had adapted. I was keen to know the details. Itching to meet the family and,

Doremi, if, that was her. I turned to check the search engine for Mr. Murthy - her father. Yes, that was uncle. He looked tired, haggard but still had the same kind eyes. And Doremi; omigosh, looked way different from the image that popped up before my eyes. Gone were the oiled plaits and bug eyed look. I leaned back in my chair to take a deep breath. This new avatar, I definitely liked!

It was providence that forced me to handover the resignation letter a few weeks ago. I was sick and tired of the corporate life. My life and work were on the same level. Ambition and remuneration had taken a backseat a long while ago. Delhi had begun to irk me. I was beginning to question where I was heading. I did not have a life. Neither were friends or companionship on my wish list. I did not have the time for anything, leave alone introspect. I was beginning to call myself a bore and suspected that the ugly snickers behind my back went along the same lines. The truth was, I was saturated. Exhausted. Nothing excited me. Not even the money or my high profile job. I had become part of the monotony. I was stuck in a rut and needed a change. Frankly, the letter stirred something in me. It was time to call my agent for a weekend ticket to the 'Kanhaganj' of the south. And hoped that this phase would pass. I would let my instinct guide me.

*

A curt information in the form of a mail had been sent requesting for an extra day off clubbed with the weekend. Knowing the management, I'm sure that they would agree to whatever I asked for. I was tired of watching their hangdog expression and tell myself, 'Just this one year. There won't be a next'.

Expertly packing formal shirts and a suit for the interview, I included a shirt and *veshti*[8] ensemble should an informal visit to the home be included. Packing was a non-strenuous affair as I had been doing this for most of my working life anyway. I could pack and unpack stuff from a suitcase with my eyes closed. Travel time was three hours along with a few more of those stuck in the choking traffic. I was waiting to fly away from the smog.

Touchdown followed by customs check was a breeze. I followed the taxi driver bearing my name on the placard to his ambassador car. The ride was a silent affair as I was immersed in my thoughts. Nervousness coupled with trepidation was something that I was unaccustomed to for a long time now. I felt hesitant and unsure. Taking out a cigarette, I rolled down the window and proceeded to calm myself.

The structure that loomed before me was not a grandiose one. It was a cement and brick plastered double storied building. The yard in front teemed with lush greenery. Young fruit bearing trees stood discreetly among the larger shrubs close to the compound wall. I paid the fare and observed the view from within the enclosure after walking in through the open gates. A khaki clad native, presumably the watchman, came running to close the gate, offer his apologies and carry my suitcase. I watched him mutter non-stop without a clue as to what was being conveyed but at my indication that I had come to see the Big Man here, he barked out a laugh and motioned that here; a 'respected woman' ran the show. *'Periyamma'*[16] he repeated twice encouraging me to repeat the word. I nodded to show that I had understood and followed him into the cool interior. Ceiling fans whirred at high speed all along the long corridor. There were men, women and children of all ages and sizes, sitting on the plastic chairs touching the walls as well as a few others hunched over and sitting on the floor with outstretched legs. All glances swiveled upon my entry and the entire group rose with palms folded with some bowing low and muttering, 'Doctor aiyya'.

Taken aback at this response, I espied the board that said, 'Murthy-Managing Director' and walked in through the door. Inside the room was uncle, head bowed and writing furiously on a notepad. Hearing my tap on the door, he looked up confused. A tall man in a suit was a rarity in this part of the world. As his gaze took me in and rested on my face, comprehension dawned. 'Manu,' he said. Uncle got up from his position and came to enfold me in a hug. After giving me a chair and a glass of water, he enquired about the journey and my travel plans. Nodding at my answer, he stood up abruptly. "It's time you meet the person who is the life and soul of this place."

"Periyamma?" I enquired and uncle laughed. We walked on to the next room. It was marked, 'waiting room'. Here, a few women sat on chairs and a weighing machine stood at one end of the room. Rapid fire muttering at the woman who was having her son weighed, followed by a volley of instruct-tion to the nurse standing by the Chief Doctor's side. Clad in a sari with hair clipped at the back, I would recognize that voice any-where. This was Doremi; Periyamma and, Chief Doctor all rolled in one; the lady who ran the show. I could feel all the pieces fall into place and a happy grin split my face wide open.

*

Dr. Sagarika gave me a cursory look and ushered us out of the room. Her consultation room was at the end of the corridor. A well-appointed room, it had a raised bed that served to check on patients who required a lie-down. I looked around and noted that the walls were bare save for a calendar that was printed in a South Indian language. Malayalam, I learnt later. As we sat facing her, I was struck by the changes. She had mellowed but there was a steely glint in her gaze. Aware that I was staring hard, uncle cleared his throat. This was an interview, I reminded myself.

Doctor Sagarika observed me for a moment and said, "Manu," to which, I smiled.

She quickly corrected herself, "Mr. Manu," My shoulders began to shake.

Catching the drift, uncle joined in.

Sagarika grinned broadly and continued, "Mr. Manavlal Yadav, welcome to M/s Sagarika General Hospital."

The thaw had softened. The humble beginning of the hospital was narrated, my duties outlined, there was no Periyaaiyya running the show except for uncle, I was assured with a smile. I felt chastened and sheepish at the last remark.

The remuneration would be a fraction of what I was getting but it would be improved every year. As demands far outweighed the needs, I would be required on site 24/7. This was a hospital with a mission. Personal gains were not in consideration. Service to the needy was to be the outcome. It seemed to be a personal issue with the Murthys' I gathered.
I found myself agreeing to everything that she said. I do not know what came upon me. The money and living style were issues I was not overly concerned about. I was sick of the life I led anyway. But, there was a hitch. The language.

"I understand," replied Dr. S to that. Suppressing a smile, she stole a look at uncle and looked directly at me to say, "For that, I have the best teacher at hand. His patient guidance will help you learn the language effectively. I know so because he was my teacher as well during my school years," Giving a tap on the bell with her forefinger, she asked the peon to call Murugan and introduce him to Manaiyya.

*

Manaiyya—my new name. Her choice.

Not Ray. Not Allen. It seemed that I was stuck with this version for now. My shoulders drooped and I got up to meet this 'Murugan' under whose care, I was to be assigned.

Jaw dropping shock! To say that I was flabbergasted was an understatement. I had been neatly cornered. This Murugan was just an old, bent villager! The same one who had muttered non-stop and insisted on my addressing the Periyamma the right way. How was he supposed to guide me? Was this the break from the corporate life that I had hankered for? This seemed to be the total opposite of what I was doing so far. Trust my instincts, my foot!

Everything seemed to be happening incredibly fast. The trip, this job, Uncle and Periyamma, and now, this Mururgan; son of a gun!

I trudged wearily behind him as he smiled and shook his head at me all the while, rapidly firing away phrases or names; I am not sure which came first. He led me outside to the garden and pointed at the trees, shrubs, all the greenery muttering and nodding at me. I waved my right hand at him and gestured that I did not understand. "Hindi," I said loudly. "Hindi. No Tamil." Murugan was nonplussed and stared at me for several seconds. Then off he rushed inside to confer with his boss madam and Periyaaiyya, I suppose. I was tired, hot and, hungry. Bundling my suit under my arm, I waited under the shade of a towering Peepal (sacred fig) tree that stood outside of the compound, for Murugan to return.

*

The three days extended to a week later, ten days. Finally, I called and informed the management that they were to count me out. I was going to try my luck in the land of the 'madrasis'. I could imagine the shocked faces and the hushed whispers. Stray comments about *Manavlalji*[18] making a bad move, jibes on ruination of the career, and so on.

I had decided to take the risk. Plunge in. I could fathom that the voice held me captive. Of course, it was not just that. I recognized the pull. But, the thought of going back to my penthouse depressed me. I had wanted to break out. To rebel. And I was being given the chance on a golden platter. If this was meant to end in regret, so be it. I would indulge in that at a later date. Not now. Not when the intrigue was just beginning to beckon.

I stayed as a guest at the Murthys' home. The house was practically empty with uncle and Dr. S at the hospital throughout the day. Aunty was at home supervising home cooked meals for the family. The food was packed in steel boxes along with copper canisters that contained drinking water and buttermilk and was sent to the hospital in a beat up car by mid-afternoon every day. The amount that was cooked was gargantuan. Since I subsisted on a roti or two and a sabzi, the array of dishes confounded me. Rice, sambar, *rasam*[25], up to two vegetable dishes—seasoned or steamed and accompanied by a gravy-based relish, yoghurt, a chutney, pickle, *appalams*[30], and a sweet. The meals were served on plantain leaves. About ten numbers were cut every day, rubbed clean, tied with string and dispatched along with the containers. Most often, Murugan; yes, my tutor and general helper, landed at noon to handle the arduous task. The heat drained me and I needed time out between shifts. There were practically no shifts to speak of. So, I had to work up a schedule for practically everything, which seemed monstrously arduous given the fact that oversimplification was a matter of principle. There were no concrete rules that were followed in this part of the town.

The afternoon ritual thus, became a done deed. I regularly caught the ride in the car to the house with Murugan and the driver chortling away at my struggle in mastering the language. Thamizh was the local language but the Murthy family spoke fluent Malayalam at home. It was often no-man's land in my case. Tut-tutting at my condition, aunty would often remonstrate her husband and daughter and, that arrogant ass-Murugan. The switchover to Hindi would be a welcome respite, save for the bumbling gardener.

Aunty would now wait for my arrival to share the day's happenings while we ate. I was allowed a siesta of a full two hours, her diktat that none dared oppose. Her notion was that, I was working too hard for someone this new. Uncle hemmed and hawed at this while Doremi sulked. It was as if the four of us had bonded and functioned like a well-oiled unit. Murugan also displayed mild reverence, which was quite humbling considering his relationship with the family. Through him, I came to know and understand events of the yesteryears that had guided the family to its current exalted state. The entire population swore by Periyamma's name. She was the blessed one. No one could take her place. Murugan's Sagupaapaa was a phenomenon. And his Maariyamman had a hand in that.

*

Days flew by and so did the months. The first six though, were tumultuous with confusion reigning supreme. The entire system followed the coveted, 'first come, first serve' routine. Breaks and shifts were unheard of and I marveled at the dedication and energy put in by Team Periyamma. Knowing that my being was here for a reason, meetings were held and it was decided that the organization and management of the hospital would have a separate team of dedicated personnel. Dr. S would retain her team of doctors including the young intern Chandrashekhar, who would take care of all professional aspects such as diagnosis, laboratory, minor surgeries and the outpatient ward. A dispensary was included within the compound so that patients could avail of medicines as per the directive received from the concerned doctors. Travelling a kilometer away from the hospital to purchase the medicines could be avoided and the time saved was an additional advantage as well.

I, Manavlal Yadav was formally proclaimed as head of the Admin department. The revenue and logistics department now began to show a semblance of order. Several women were hired as ayahs from the vicinity and Murugan as the team lead, wore his badge with pride whilst conferring with them and orienting them on their duties. Nurses and Doctors began to follow the shift system with mandatory breaks in between. Two additional vehicles and an ambulance were purchased through bank loans and it was proposed that residential quarters for the personnel to stay on site be erected. I was able to meet and convince the very banks that had rejected the eminent Doctor's application for the rapid changes to be implemented in a smooth manner. It was thus that, I moved out of the Murthys' residence and began to live in a portion of the quarters allocated as per my designation. The daily lunch trips and weekend visits to the home continued on a regular basis. I began to feel as though I finally found my calling. The void within me, I had identified as yearning for a family. Something that I had thought was not destined for me, now seemed to be within my reach. Nights heightened my anxiousness. Time seemed to be stagnant. Dawn dissipated the tense moments. I had wasted years living the high life and now, not a moment was to be thrown away. Mr. Fancy Pants had turned ardent admirer. Gone were the days where my sneers would crumple and deflate egos. Manavlal Yadav now craved to hear that voice, the smile that came along his way and the intense look that turned his insides to a quivering mass of happiness.

It was obvious to all but Periyamma that a rank newcomer had crept into the ranks of fervent admirer. The debatable point was when would either of the two realize or accept what was meant to be.

*

With the hospital running successfully, fame came calling. The very first invite addressed to Dr. Sagarika M.B.B.S, M.D. for the prestigious All India Medical Conference that was to be held across four weekdays in Bangalore was received. As preparations for the event were made with feverish excitement, I felt my heart plummet. Four long days! Now, the days would seem as intolerable as the nights. Summoning up the guts I decided to take the bull by the horns. Walking into her room, I cleared my throat. The Doctor and team were huddled around her table engaged in what seemed to be, a serious discussion. I cleared my throat rather loudly yet again. There was a sudden hush and heads turned in my direction. I felt a flush travelling from the neckline of my shirt to my face. (It was the heat, I told myself. The ceiling fan needed to be replaced.)

I had to continue now that I had her attention. In a raspy voice, tongue grating against teeth, I rushed on, "Doctor S, your tickets have been booked." She nodded in affirmation.

Sweat trickled down my temples. "Does the invite extend to two? I know Bangalore well. I could show you around once the conference is done with." I noted the smirks but strained to hear her reply. It was as though all the cells of my body were screaming for attention. After a hesitant pause came the answer, "Well. I have never had a vacation since I started work here, Manavlal Yadavji. Guess this would be a good time to start." The room erupted in cheers and whistles. This was obviously a date that had been long in coming. All the members stood up, clapped and watched us; their heads of the department nodded and smiled stupidly at each other. I felt relief wash over me. It was an idiotic move I knew. One that would go down as part of the local lore but right now, all I needed was a glass of water and a chair to support my weak legs.

*

How had Manaiyya managed to convince Periyamma was the question everyone had on his or her lips. It was a miracle. Doctoramma needed a life; a life outside of the hospital and its routine. She needed a man who would cushion her from the world's ills. Someone who would comfort, cajole and, calm her down. Take on the responsibilities that she had had to shoulder for so long. Her aged parents needed a break. This was preordained. Manaiyya had come to Ravirajapuram at the right time.

The conference went well considering the initial hiccups. Barring the time the car broke down on the highway and taking the wrong route towards Mysore, frenetic pointing and waving of hands towards the correct diversion to be made to reenter Bangalore by concerned locals, reaching the venue an hour behind schedule not forgetting, the misplacing of notes for the presentation which was retrieved from the bag reserved for toiletries in the nick of time, Dr. Sagarika managed to redeem herself.

In the meantime, I managed to corner a bellboy to enquire about popular hotspots in and around the garden city. The boy knew passable Hindi and therefore, I stuck to him like a leech. Directions to Cubbon Park, the Lalbagh Botanical garden, Tipu's fort, The Bangalore Palace, and, Bannerghetta National Park were hand drawn on individual pieces of paper and I gave the driver time out from his duties. Sagarika seemed slightly dubious at the start but tempered down and accepted my grand role as friend-cum-guide without comment. I'm sure that she noticed my controlled state of agitation, the erratic beat of the pulse at the base of my throat, and my clammy hands when I helped her step down from the stool of the self-serving canteen we were having our lunch in. I did not want her to beat a hasty retreat though I wanted her for myself as well. How could one balance such a fine divide? After two days of sightseeing, I was tired of the pretense. We were not kids anymore and time was running out. I needed to talk straight and quit acting like the lovelorn kid with the massive crush. We were on top of the Nandi hills looking at the view ahead of us in silence. The atmosphere was serene. The climb towards the *Anjaneya*[22] temple went well. After the obligatory circumambulation and our legs screaming for attention, we sat close to each other content. Our tired feetneeded the rest.. I turned to watch the soft wind brush tendrils of hair against her face. My hand went of its own volition to tuck them behind her ear. Sagarika seemed deep in thought and did not seem to mind the action. After a pause, she said, "I assume you know."

"Know what?" was my query.

"Don't play the innocent," she snapped. "Either Amma or Murugan must have given you the entire spiel."

"What exactly do you want me to tell you, Sagarika?" I asked her in a soft tone. "Violation at an early age doesn't entail living out the whole of one's life as a monk. Nothing was your fault. You have everyone's love including mine," I added. Sagarika looked at me deeply and turned to gaze at the view once more. She sighed with a shudder. Our hands reached out and enjoined in a firm clasp. Her voice was slow, hesitant sometimes, and I was loath to interrupt her as she spoke. Her trust in me was what mattered. She conversed in Hindi. We always did so when we were together. That extended the feel of intimacy.

Words poured out of her like a torrent. Feelings of guilt, grief, suppressed emotions that had formed a tight ball inside. Of the raw ache that threatened to explode... her hatred of Velan, the abandonment of Kurinji, words overflowed unceasingly until she was spent. It took the best part of the night and we lay against the grass, watching the stars and the rising dawn until it was light. The temple formed a bright silhouette behind us and we were reminded of the grace that remained.

On reaching the hotel we proceeded to checkout. The driver was sent back to the hospital at Ravirajapuram. The vehicle was a necessary utility and its continued absence would throw the transport section into frenzied disarray. I enclosed a polite note to uncle that stated we would be back after a week or so as the Doctor madam was enjoying her impromptu vacation. We checked into a suite at the luxurious Taj West End. Nothing was too grand for my Doremi. It was time for me to sweep her off her feet.

*

Languorous days followed. We explored the city and its numerous by-lanes. The city's famed lakes sought interested visitors like us. We walked through busy intersections, haggled our way across shops off Commercial street, licked through ice lollies that were sold by vendors in carts that tinkled, discovered eateries that served delicious biryani, gibbered and jabbered away to our heart's content. I suppose that Sagarika was able to drop her air of reserve and once done, became the free spirit that she always had been. I fervently hoped that all her demons had been laid to rest.

We spoke of the future. Of her hesitation to be renamed a Yadav. The sarcasm bounced off me. She was Periyamma to all and uncle her father, was Periyaaiyya. So, I was doomed to remain Manaiyya. My mock despondency was laughed at.

We discovered ourselves just as we explored the city. All those delicious nooks and corners, wondrous moments that entailed gasps of pleasure and shy abandonment often cloaked in ambient bliss. I couldn't imagine life beyond this woman. Her happiness in all things small or big made me realize in a huge way just how worthwhile my existence had become.

*

We returned to Ravirajapuram as man and wife. Of course, our entry into the town was conveyed to the entire community within minutes. Sagu said that it reminded her of the African drum message-relay-system she had read about in the Phantom comics. How the people did this, we had absolutely no clue but we, in turn, gave them the biggest surprise of their lives. As we alighted from the car, hands clasped together, with a garland of flowers around our necks and the red spot on Sagu's hairline signifying her marital status; our status, the crowd was stunned into silence. Murugan was the first to comprehend and turning towards the group exclaimed, "Our Periyamma had returned. Returned as a bride." The crowd roared in delight. Periyaaiyya beamed in happiness. Murugan and Co. began a series of steps to the rhythmic beat of impromptu drums. The ayahs welcomed us as a couple with the traditional 'aarti' which constituted a silver platter containing handfuls of rice, flower petals and, the all-important lamp that was lit and moved in a clockwise direction around the couple to ward off evil influences. A pinch of rice was then thrown above the head of the Doctoramma symbolizing fertility followed by the flower petals. Red vermillion was applied on our foreheads and we were then allowed to enter the hospital premises. In an hour's time, someone had arranged for sweets to be distributed to everyone.

The phone was ringing non-stop and the receptionist was beginning to look exhausted. Periyaaiyya informed everyone that a grand feast would be arranged at the Murthy's residence the day after and that the entire town was invited. There was no time to print out invites and it was understood that the word-of-mouth system would reign supreme on this occasion as well. Sagu and I exchanged a quick look. This indeed, was the Indian variation on the African Drum Technique. Extremely cost effective it would seem and, lightning quick as well!

*

I was being given the second-class treatment but frankly speaking, I did not mind. I knew that Doctoramma came ahead of anything in these people's lives and I was envious of the fact that so much love and respect could be targeted towards a single lady and that was solely brought about on account of her dedicated efforts. Sagu's parents and Murugan were the happiest of the lot for obvious reasons. They felt that her life was complete only now and that this was the time that they could leave the running of the hospital in my capable hands. Chandru would be a major player as well. Uncle and aunty hinted as much. The same evening at the Murthy's residence, I outlined my plan towards expansion of the hospital eventually converting it into a charitable group that would cover the needs of patients coming from afar and not just the Ravirajapuram population. A palliative unit would also be included in the grand scheme of things. These were ideas discussed during our Bangalore trip, I explained. Uncle, aunty and Chandrashekhar listened and nodded with pride. It was a huge achievement and they were just beginning to comprehend the vastness of it with awe. I also announced that we would shift to our new home close to the hospital once it was ready. I hoped they would not think that I was taking their daughter away from them. Rather, it was the opposite. It was time, she thought of a life independent of others. Being a family meant that certain routines would change. Change for the better. Never in my dreams did I think that the palliative unit that put into action would now be used to serve the very person who had made it possible. It was an unacceptable thought.

*

A day to go before the celebrations began. We were ordered to stay at home. Work was off-limits for two days until after the end of festivities. Aunty was a cyclone of activity. The menu for the feast was set as per norms followed in Kerala. It would be a vegetarian affair. A canopy was constructed in the front yard and mounds of vegetables were sorted and diced as per requirement. It was meant to be a traditional big fat wedding even though the bride and groom were well past their prime but for the family and the general public, this was the 'one' occasion where the celebration was considered to be their moral duty. It was their Doctoramma and Manaiyya for heaven's sake.

We were informed that visitors were scheduled to arrive from Gramayur; Murugan's village. Sagupaapaa was the apple of his eye and his family and extended relatives would board the evening bus to bless the couple on time. Also poised to attend were people from neighboring towns upon whom had been graced, the good Doctoramma's benevolence.

For a moment I thought of the sad, lonely life I had had, in Delhi. The penthouse and car I had disposed of long ago. It was God's will that brought me here. I felt blessed to be part of this love. To be called as the magan (son) instead of marumagan (son-in-law) was something that I cherished. We did not spend much on ourselves. What flowed in was spent to ensure that the lives and families of our team of dedicated workers were suitable enriched. The development of the hospital into a massive structure that would offer its service to all headed by our son Chandrashekhar would be the legacy that we, as a family would leave behind at Ravirajapuram. I walked in to check on Sagu who was being cossetted by women in preparation for the next big day. She hated that, I knew. It was time to pull her out.

Shooing away the ladies took some time. They were reluctant to leave even though their Manaiyya had requested for a time out with his wife. I was fairly fluent in Thamizh by now so the early simpers and giggles at my awful accent had disappeared.

Sagu seemed pensive. It turned out that she was thinking about the Zenana. They had lost contact after the Malayapuram visit. It would be nice if she could see them all again. To let them know that she was OK. I was quiet and held her hand. All that was left of her school days was a single black and white picture with the five of them huddled together under the canvas awning of the Archie bookshop. I had imagined them from Sagu's account of her Silver Flower Hr. Sec. school days. There was only a day to go and no way to get in touch with any of them. It was a shame. The girls would have been ecstatic.

*

Custom demanded that the important day begin with a visit to the temple. It was thus that we visited the temple of Siva in the adjacent town at the crack of dawn. Although Sagu was averse to the idea, she acquiesced to the wishes of her pious mother who had remained her protective shadow throughout. As she (I now called her amma and Uncle, *appa*[20]) remarked to me during the ride, "I chose to be the shadow around my daughter. This was to ensure that no ills befell her at any time. Would any mother wish for her offspring to be inflicted in this manner? My child, my Sagu has had to undergo so much at such a tender age. This journey has been a rite through fire for all concerned. We have been struck upon and molded by the same force of nature. Until you arrived, no one had the temerity to interrupt my child's will or the calling of her choice. I chose to be her shield, an invisible one at that! One that would absorb all the negativity not allow entry within its space." She took a deep breath and continued, "My obligation as of this moment will lose its rigidity. That's a conscious decision I have taken. You, my son will take that place. I shall only be a passive force from this day. My temple visit is to convey this to the Lord." Sagu's mother paused, closed her eyes and, murmured the Lord's name under her breath.

I was awestruck. Awed at the devotion displayed by a mother to ensure that her child would remain unharmed. Awed at the responsibility I had been given albeit, discreetly. Awed that a family stayed together through thick and thin for this long just to nurture and protect. Awed that such an honor had come my way, that I had been accepted as one among them. Sagu had chosen me and they had simply accepted. Exhilaration would be the term I would choose to use at this moment. My life was complete. My goals were clear and visible. I looked at the bobbing heads of Chandrashekhar, Appa and Murugan in the front seat of the car and, Sagu and Amma with me on either side observing the still dark view. Emotion gripped my throat. I felt hot tears blind my eyes. I thanked Lord Siva in advance for having bought me here from Delhi.

*

We were exhausted upon our return. There was, however, not a minute to be wasted. A change of clothes after the customary bath following which, a mandatory meet-and-greet session would demand the newly-weds' attention. Gulping down tender coconut water from glasses, we sped to the washrooms.

A huge crowd of attendees had arrived and was waiting patiently to convey their good wishes and blessings. Customary gifts included sacks of rice, coconuts, plantains, all kinds of fruits, mounds of jaggery, cash, mattresses, metal almirahs, cement and iron rods from a hardware shop owner, and the sale deed of a small plot of land adjacent to the hospital made out in the couple's name by the generous Pannayar of a neighboring district. The storeroom of the house was full to overflowing and the gifts were then stacked in the open backyard. Sweat coursed heavily down the bodies of the Bride and Groom. The humidity coupled with the heavy attire offered little help against rising body heat and tiredness. It was as the crowds thinned that Sagu noticed a small group seated a little away from the dais. They had been served the customary drinks and now waited patiently for the file to end, to take their turn. Intent stares met with puzzlement before realization dawned. It was her Zenana. They had come to meet her. Lord of lords, her deepest wish had come true!

Sagu tugged at Manu and hopped down the dais. Her friends had covered the space in a few strides and it was as if the girls were back in Oothukudi again. Laughs, shrieks and hugs enfolded the four in a big cloud of happiness. Appa was the one to bring them together, apparently. He had shot off a telegram conveying the happy news to Marge and Shruthi a few hours after Manu and Sagu returned from Bangalore. The telegram was addressed to their Oothukudi address and he had fervently prayed for them to get the message and round up Ratna as well. His Sagu would be the happiest, he knew. None of the gifts would match up to a reunion that would bring the families together as well. The girls hugged Appa and fell at the feet of Amma. As the mutual tears flowed, Amma told them, "Let's not shed any more tears. This is a happy occasion. We should feast now and later, talk to our heart's content." It was in a lighter vein that the friends shared the repast making an occasional jibe at the indulgent and smiling groom; yours truly!

*

Life had treated the trio and their families quite well. Ratna was an assistant Professor at a government college in Pollachi. She was married to a small time businessman and had a daughter who was an exact replica of her! It was astounding to the group who wondered privately as to how she could have managed such a herculean task. Ratna being Ratna smiled and grinned at her husband. It was evident that they would exchange notes at a later date.

Shruthi had two kids, a boy and a girl. The two had completed their high school education from the Silver Flower Hr. Sec. School. and were familiar with the escapades of their mother and friends. Shruthi had proudly taken them around to all their favorite haunts and the family thus felt as though they were visiting them for the nth time rather than the first! Shruthi was the only one among us who was still based in Oothukudi having inherited her parents flat. As predicted several years ago, she led a content and happy life.

Margie had identical twin boys. She worked three days from home and her days were packed. Her husband travelled a lot so it was up to her to manage the home and the kids. She seemed harried but game to work things through. The never-give-up-attitude coupled with pitchforks of salt helped her rough it out. Financially, Marge seemed to be the best settled of the lot. Of course, there was no comparing with their Sagu who seemed to be light years ahead of them all. And what of Deenanna, I casually enquired of Marge. Major

Deendayal Xavier served in the Indian Army and it suited his disposition quite well. Marge would relay the news to him and she was sure that he would make a trip out here to meet his favorite gal pal accompanied by his family. There were oohs and aahs at this and tales of past fistfights were recounted. The twins regaled the group with a passable imitation of their uncle's blustery approach and mannerisms.

It was time to introduce our son, Chandrashekhar to the Zenana. Incredulous looks would follow I'm sure, but there would be a polite wait for us to spill the beans. As Sagu called out for Chandru, the sight of the tall, strapping lad left the friends bemused. Placing a hand on his shoulder she continued, "Meet Chandru, Dr. Chandrashekhar; upcoming oncologist and soon to be Director of the Sagarika Charitable Group of Hospitals." Chandru fidgeted at this unnecessary show of pomp and smiled at everyone politely. "He was raised in the U.S.A. where he completed his schooling. For his higher education, he chose to come down, live with us and complete his internship. He's this Doctoramma's right hand." She indicated herself with her free hand. "Meet my son. Our son," she amended instantly catching my eye. Appa and Amma proudly beamed from the doorway. Core Z looked impressed and baffled. Chandru knew what was coming and quickly excused himself, rushing into the house.

Sagarika then remarked, "I know exactly what is going through your minds. We have hardly been in touch so it's but natural that you are confused."

"Chandru is my brother's stepson. They are in Texas, have been there for ages now. Green card holders and all that. But this boy always had a soft spot for me and likewise. So, when he was old enough to speak his mind and indicate his career preferences, his parents were duly informed. Fortunately for everyone concerned, the idea was wholeheartedly embraced and agreed upon. My brother and his wife have a daughter in addition to him so they did not feel pain at the parting. Moreover, they are happy that he's with his aunt and grandparents and now, Manu. Should he choose to return, they would not oppose that either, but for now, he seems to fit in rather well here, with us."

It was during this time, that Murugan walked into their midst beaming widely to loud exclamations of delight from the friends who welcomed him into their fold.

"Muruhaa Velmuruhaa, you are still stuck to your Sagu paapaa. She's not in school anymore or have you forgotten?" Marge's statement was followed by raucous laughter. At this, poor Murugan sheepishly looked down and avoided everyone's gaze.

"He's abandoned his family but never Sagu," shot out Shruthi in jest.

"Well, we have never heard from you. Remember any of us?' Marge glowered at him in mock anger to which Murugan anxiously shook his head in dismay. It seemed as if the stage was being set for a mock trial to be held with poor Murugan on one side and the friends on the other.

"He's been taking care of her for us. Something that we were meant to do." Ratna's quiet interjection cut through the gay chatter almost instantly. There was an abrupt shift in mood. A sudden dip in temperature. For a split second, the mockery had shone through. And Ratna had cut through that. Shruthi and Marge blanched in response and stood stock still. Sagu's grip on me tightened and I sensed her anguish. Ratna remained impassive almost, stoic. She had regretted uttering the words but she was right and they all knew it.

Deep down, they had borne the guilt of not being there for their Sagu and the wound had festered and deepened.. It had neither reduced nor been redeemed.

Only dear Murugan had displayed unconditional love and loyalty towards their loved one. He had a family, just like them but he had chosen to balance his priorities well. And they chose to poke and prod at him in a way, to stymie the pain. It was unintentional in the beginning but the tremor had begun to resurface.

The four friends faced each other and felt the years being stripped away.

It felt as though they were transported back in time and all the moments that bound them together flashed before their eyes. A raw ache balled in their throats and threatened to burst out of their very souls. Helpless tears gathered begging for penitence.

I understood the frailty of the situation and knew that peace had to be made. Nudging my wife towards the three, instantly broke the spell.

The four gathered together in a tight circle and sobbed as one. Murugan stood by, wringing his hands in helplessness. Sagu's parents were glad that the mend had been made. The disjoint had been remedied. The zenana was back in action although it was now saddled with individual responsibilities but the cradle of love that had held it together, remained undiminished.

The families were allotted their rooms within the Murthy household while the four chattered on. The children were spirited away by the ayahs to be shown around the place and pampered with goodies and eatables. Amma was supervising the packing of gargantuan gift bags as part of the give-away tradition from the pile received as the friends were scheduled to travel back the next day. Individual gunny bags filled with sweets, fruits, coconut, and other assorted items were being readied in the backyard of the house. With the kids running helter-skelter and tidying up of the front yard once the few remaining guests had left, the place was a mad house of activity.

Meeting Murugan's family members made me happy. It was also an eye-opener. They were attired in their best and stood diffidently around the elder member of their family. It was evident that they had faced lives of strife and I resolved to ease their hardship in the best possible manner that I could. No one questioned my choice of action. I was free to undertake whatever I thought was in the best interests of the organization. Sagu and Appa had begun this journey, yet, their trust in me remained true.

They had granted me a life. No arguments on that one.

*

I had noticed the sudden loss of energy, lack of appetite, the sweaty palms, vacant unfocused look and attributed them to the punishing work schedule. It was when we were getting dressed for work that I noticed the marked delay in her emergence from the bathroom. As I called out for her, I felt my impatience growing. Ten minutes later, I went in to investigate.

Bedroom- empty.
Bathroom, locked from inside.

After several knocks and calling out, I shouted out to the driver who rushed in, concerned. Together, we broke open the door. On the floor lying unconscious was, our Doctoramma. Heaving, we carried her to the bed and switched on the overhead fan. Kripan, our driver, went down to get a glass of water. Gently patting her cheeks and murmuring her name, I felt her eyelids flutter. As she struggled to rise, I supported her against the pillows and gave her the glass of water that Kripan had bought. I indicated that he was to wait downstairs and keep the matter to himself. As the sound of his steps receded, I turned and looked at Sagu. She smiled at my look of concern. "Don't be such a paapaa. I won't disappear, Manu." Her tittering incensed me and I asked her to rest for the day.

I called in every two hours but after the third call, her tone sounded petulant. "Either you stay here by my side or, stop the pestering." I had to put an end to my concern after that. It was not a big deal but the first time almost always seems like the biggest hurdle. Doctoramma treated others. She did not need the looking after. Hence, the concern seemed unnecessary. I diverted my attention to the head of the ayahs. Her complaint was towards the logistics manager who had disrespected one of her charges. The woman was stout, short, bristling with vehemence and was clad in an orange sari flecked with brown and red spots. An enormous *bindi*[21] flashed the warning sign from between her eyebrows. I sighed. The day just didn't seem to end.

My apprehensions were laid to rest as I gazed at Sagu late in the evening. She seemed refreshed, eyes sparkling with joy as she guided me to the garden, to our favorite nook. Here, she had readied a table with iced tea and tidbits. A chicken curry was simmering on the gas stove, so I was to freshen up and come back here to join her for dinner. The rice was just about done along with a fresh salad on the side that had chopped onions, finely diced green chilies, tomato and, cucumber, followed by puffed rice that would be tossed in mustard oil. The last two ingredients were remnants of my north eastern upbringing that Sagu reminisced upon but I was now, chiefly, a rice-sambar-rasam man. The conversion was complete!

We had reverted to our normal routine. Get up early, walk around the colony, bathe, dress and, rush to work. Dinner was always together, at home, and we made it a point to wait and check on areas that needed scheduling. The talk kept us focused and aware of most nitty-gritty's associated with the running of the hospital. The construction was almost complete and we were in the process of getting the organization converted into a charitable trust. Henceforth, the clinic that Dr. Sagarika had started out with would be known as M/s Sagarika Group of Charitable Hospitals. It was way beyond what she had hoped for and dreamt of and I was glad to be a part of the endeavor. The challenge had revitalized me. I was glad to have escaped the rut that I had once considered all-important. Chandrashekhar was also working his way upwards. The lad was studious and dedicated like his aunt. They were a well-matched pair. That the boy revered his aunt beyond words was a given. Dr. Chandrashekhar Gurumurthy would shoulder the legacy he would eventually be handed over. There was no doubt about that.

The second episode came to my notice six months later. It was quite by chance that I found her slumped over her desk and unresponsive. I did not know whether this was the second singular episode or whether Sagu was aware of few others (I hoped not) but I decided to take matters into my own hands. I made enquiries and despite her vehemence, we travelled by car to Chennai the next day. My target was to reach the Apollo Hospital and admit Sagu for a detailed check-up. I had known that she would have wanted to keep the matter under wraps and that, I did. Under the pretext of having to visit certain professionals in Chennai with Doctoramma accompanying me, Kripan drove at a sedate pace. He was the next best person that I trusted after Murugan. Good old Murugan would not be able to take in the news without a certain amount of lamentation added to which, his physical frailty might not withstand the stress. I wanted to avoid a twin tragedy at any cost.

I felt gloomy and depressed. Kripan had sensed the tension and therefore, avoided the small talk.

"I'm sure it's nothing, Manu. You fret over small matters. It could be low BP or anemia for all you know," offered Sagu in a reassuring tone.

"Of course, you are right. You are the renowned Doctor," I retorted in anger. "You would know for certain if it was a trivial matter. Can I have your word on that?"

Sagu remained quiet. Watching her withdrawn expression, I felt my heart sink. "I have arranged for a master health check-up at Apollo. That way we would get to know." There was no response from her.

"Doremi," I placed my hand on her knee and shook it slightly. "Please don't scare me. For your sake, I'll think that you are anemic or something," my voice trailed to a whisper. I noticed Kripan watching us through the rear view mirror. His eyes had dilated. Probably alarm, I decided. "Look ahead and drive man," I instructed him tersely and he obediently looked forward, shifting gears.

*

As we neared the hospital, it was decided that a stopover at the *Annadaan Bhojanalaya*[23] by mid-afternoon was the need of the hour. The outfit was a famous vegetarian restaurant and Indians all over the world swore by its hospitality and quality of cuisine.

Sagu declined to eat stating that she did not feel hungry. She asked a cup of their famed filter coffee and a plate of *idlis*[24].

Kripan and I would normally settle for the South Indian *Thali*[31]. This had about 15 varieties of dishes that were served continuously until your gut threatened to overflow. But today was not the day for a feast. And so, I downed two cups of the filter coffee and watched Kripan picking on a dosa. Sagarika was watching us in silence. Following my visit to the restroom, I sat beside her with a sigh.

I thought that I felt her stir and turned to look at her. The woman had waited for the opportune moment. My vulnerable side was exposed and my guard was strewn all over the place and that was when she announced, "Just to keep you in the loop, I would like you to know what is to be expected at Apollo."

This was so unexpected that my antenna shot up in alarm. Sagu continued, "I would be examined, my symptoms looked into, which would then be followed by a simple neurological examination. If I am suspected to have a tumor or the prognosis is unclear about what's causing these symptoms, they may refer me to a brain and nerve specialist for further investigation."

She watched my expression of shock with sympathy and continued mercilessly; "The GP or neurologist may then subject me to a battery of tests for problems associated with tumor of the brain. This may involve testing of my arm and leg strength, reflexes, such as knee-jerk reflex, hearing and vision, skin sensitivity, balance and co-ordination, memory and mental agility using simple questions or arithmetic. The neurologist may also recommend one or more of the tests such as a CT scan, an MRI scan and possibly an EEG. Now, if a tumor is suspected, **a biopsy** may be carried out to establish the type and the most effective treatment for the same." She stopped and lightly slapped the side of my face. "Manu, I already know what it is going to be but for my sake, please be strong." Her voice was a plea. "My suspicions were aroused but it is normal for any practicing Doctor to ignore what goes on inside of them. I made myself busier and that exhausted me." I looked on at her limply. It was peak hours and the waiter stopped by our table furtively, hoping that the bill would be settled. We ignored him as Sagu continued with a self-deprecating smile, "All I had to do was speak to Chandru but I cannot. I cannot bear to watch the sympathy all over again. I want things to be as they were." I tried to come up with a suitable retort but words failed me. I felt as though I was punched in the gut.

She knew. She suspected. And we were left out.
We were the façade centered on the helium.

There had to be a way.

Doctors were too logical. I did not want to be the grim reaper as well.

"Let's move. I don't want to be late," I hoped that my voice didn't sound strangulated. Placing a few notes inside the bill folder I walked out. Scrolling through the contact list on my phone for Kripan's number, I felt Sagarika stand close to me. I could smell her perfume. It took a lot of effort to not turn and look at the pretty face. I did not want to see worry mar her fine features. Most of it stemmed on my account. She was strong and as pliable as the bamboo that flowed and weaved with the wind. Her concern towards me bothered. And hurt. We got into the car.

As predicted, a biopsy was required. We were asked to stay for an extra day. We could leave the next evening owing to the patient's special status. The results would be mailed to us. Alternatively, a conference call could also be arranged. The third day saw us back at Ravirajapuram. Sagarika was dropped off at home and I went back to the hospital. Since it was unheard of, about Doctoramma being unavailable even for a day, I had to field queries upon queries from all and sundry that had to be patiently dealt with. It was a torturous day and despair seeped through. Never had I felt such pain. I would have to keep it all to myself and pretend that everything was normal even though it was not.

It was what Sagarika wanted.

I wanted to shout out.

Scream.

Drink myself to death and not wake up. Maintaining a pleasant exterior was excruciating.

I died a million deaths since the last forty-eight hours and counting and I was not sure that I would last long at this rate.

But at the same time, my sensible other half prodded. The logical, grasping-at-straws half. Two words surfaced and posted this in large letters - What if? And my emotional half eagerly grasped at the proffered lifeline and conjectured. What if the logical line of reasoning turned out to be incorrect? What if there was hope on the other hand? There was supposed to be a ray of sunshine at the end of the tunnel. Misery did not suit me rather; I was going to 'unfriend' this gloom. My jauntiness reappeared as I walked back home after refusing the ride back, with an extra bounce to my step. The 'what if' had offered me hope. I was not going to let go.

The mail from Apollo had arrived, the second day after we reached Ravirajapuram. It was addressed to Doctor Sagarika with a cc to me.

The bad news first - There was a tumor in the brain.

The good news – It seemed to be benign.

However, the tumor was located deep inside the brain and would be difficult to remove without damaging the surrounding tissue. In these cases, a special type of radio-therapy called stereotactic radiosurgery would have to be conducted.

"During radiosurgery, tiny beams of high-energy radiation are focused on the tumor to kill the abnormal cells," Sagu explained. "Treatment consists of one session, recovery is quick, and an overnight stay in hospital isn't usually needed."

However, she continued, "Radiosurgery is only available in a few specialized centers in India. It's only suitable for some people, based on the characteristics, location and size of the tumor. So basically, I have a fifty percent chance provided the chemo destroys the leftover cells and reconversion of the benign cells does not occur."

"Reconversion?" I asked her puzzled. "Shift to cancerous mode at a later date," she replied patiently. "All this is conjecture at this stage. There are a lot more tests that I have to undergo to be sure."

Did I feel my sensible half prod me again? I looked at Sagu in the eye and said, "Let's just assume as you say, that all this is conjecture. What if they are wrong? What if the second round of tests don't bring anything up? Would you take a break from tradition and come with me? We could hike. Breathe in fresh air. Go for a pilgrimage."

Her refusal was a slap on the face. **Damn the woman. She was smart, sexy at times, timid to the point of meekness, dedicated, a visionary, generous to a fault, painfully honest, ethical Goddess, dutiful child and wife. But when her mind was set, she could be so, so stubborn.**

I had trusted my sensible self. Thought that logic would take second place. Having to process all this alone was killing me. Better me than her. She was too important. Her piety towards the goal that she had envisaged was to be respected. I, on the other hand, needed to make a quick getaway. Lose myself into nothingness. Perhaps something would come out of this oblivion.

Manaiyya would depart silently. No one would suspect until the day was almost over. I pictured the pall of gloom amongst the hospital staff and Periyamma, glum and despondent, ensconced inside her room. That I would be missed, I was sure of but I also knew that no one would dare probe and worm their way into the void. The threshold would be visible for all to see.

*

The Shree Mata Lodging Establishment, Katra

A hot breeze wafted in from the open window. The pungent tang and the moist warmth of it fanned the gauzy pink curtains that hung from aluminum rods cut to the width of the window. Lizard droppings dotted the narrow strip of wall above the window that met the ceiling. Tiny, dry, mostly black and white crescents formed a strange pattern when closely observed. The yellow light of the incandescent bulb gave them shadows. Shadows that turned small crescents into elongated half-moons. The lizards were fearless. They crawled along the upper half of the wall and hung about on the ceilings. The open loft that was a mere ledge on the opposite end was stacked high with a stained, folded mattress, paper cartons, battered suitcases and old newspapers that were frayed and yellowed. Bits of them floated down as soon as the ceiling fan was switched on giving a surreal edge to the room. The play of dust motes, bits of paper and golden light that danced through them, seemed mesmerizing. Manu watched them lazily through half closed eyes; while he sipped from a glass that was half filled with scotch and water. The lizards formed part of the strange tableau as they gazed in silence from within the inner recesses of the loft.

Come mornings though, and the room's haphazard condition invited a barrage of abuse from the aged cleaning woman named Lakshmi. Her harried expression belied the eagerness of an escape from this stink hole. Within moments, the curtains would be pulled open, the pile of clothes on the floor scooped away, soiled bedspread whipped off the single bed, and layers of dust wiped off the table that was piled with books, notes and assorted stationary items accompanied by a single, broken chair. An old rag was rinsed in grimy water that was the accumulation of the just-completed-cleaning of the neighboring rooms. Aiming a well-placed kick at the bundled clothes heaped near the door, Lakshmi would proceed to sit on her haunches and wipe the floor in a series of arcs.

Wet arcs when dry, left arcs of grey on the floor.

The direction of the pattern changed every day depending on the point of origin. If Lakshmi had cleared the droppings from the wall using her ragged broom and then proceeded to mop, the arcs would swing from inside out much like a pattern that disappeared from view as soon as they were made on the terracotta tiled floor. This pattern suffered marked displacement especially after Manav's visit to the bathroom for completion of his morning rituals.

Wet feet left gaps in the arcs. Yawning irregular spaces that broke the symmetry.

On days that were rushed, he hardly ever noticed. Thoughtful days inclined to bouts of appreciation of Lakshmi's handiwork, made hopping between the lines a mandatory evil. Gingerly tiptoeing through with bare feet and making the last hop over the doorsill was a hard to beat feat. Crowing in victory, he would make his way to the booking office. It had been a week since he arrived. Waiting to get a place among the long list of devotees that thronged the site, his days and nights were spent in isolation and silent contemplation.

Manav had reached Katra in the Indian state of Jammu and Kashmir where the temple of *Vaishno Devi*[17] was located. While filling up the form, he had rejected the use of ponies or other modes of transportation preferring to walk all the way to the temple precinct. He wished to witness the 'aarti' ceremony that offered worship to the Goddess once before sunrise and the other, after sunset. He promised to stop consuming alcohol as soon as his booking was confirmed. Getting through the day was difficult otherwise. The office staff noting his desperation sympathized with him and advised patience. When her call would come, the timing would be just right. He missed his work, the people, his family and most of all, his Sagarika. But the pain had to be dulled. He would not return unless he was granted his wish.

The room at the lodge he was in was far from mediocre, situated inside a seedy locality. It was purely by accident that he stumbled into the cramped reception that was manned by a despondent young boy, after his unplanned exit from the railway station. How or what had brought him here, he had no idea. But it bought a semblance of order albeit gratingly into the mind-numbing pathos he was mired in. Lakshmi and her screeching routine, he welcomed. The walk around the locality filled up the mundane spaces. He had not let anyone know where he was. When and if he decided to return, he would make the call. She would wait for him. It would not be easy for her to let go. Of that he was sure.

"Come with me," he had entreated but she had refused. "This is my temple. I have known no other."

And he had sobbed. Sobbed hard. Smashed the book in hand against the glass case. Thrown a chair into a corner where it crashed into the wall, splintering into several pieces. She looked troubled but let him be, exiting the room quietly.

The next morning found him ready by the door, small bag in hand. "I have to try. Try and find my Maariyamman.

She must know that I need her now." Sagu seemed small, fragile, resigned. He continued, "Unless I'm sure, I shall not return. Promise me that you will wait." She had nodded her acquiescence to that, silent and unsmiling.

And that was how he had landed in Katra, at the base of the Trikuta hills waiting to meet the Goddess who was known to have legendary healing powers.

The tenth day visit to the office proved to be lucky. He was allowed access to the walk for the next day but a few obligatory steps had to be accomplished at first. Online checking could be completed at a nearby Internet café he was advised but before that, the purchase of the ticket from the Yatra registration center was to be effectuated. Next step, checkout from the Shree Mata Lodging Establishment, book a locker to safely place his travel bag and phone. Armed with his wallet, Manu proceeded to register his details on the Mata Vaishno Devi Shrine Board's official website and uncheck both boxes for the VIP pass that allowed special access into the temple as well as a room at the Bhawan close to the shrine. Another check of the site in the evening showed that his waiting status was now confirmed and that he had to be present at the Banganga check post situated at the foothills of the Trikuta Mountains. He wanted to walk barefoot all the way and back though it was frowned upon but not a rarity. Devotee mindsets varied and there were all kinds visiting the Mata to avail of her generous nature.

Having been assured that food and water were available along the way, Manu travelled light. The climb upwards was smooth although he could have taken the steps that were steep and allowed for quicker reach at the mid-point called 'Ardhkuari'. However, he doubted that his feet could withstand the unaccustomed terrain and preferred the gentle slant of the upward climb instead. Taking note of the mountains dotted with light snow and the chatter of the pilgrims along with devotional music and ponies trekking by his side, Manu was distracted by thoughts of a strange man he had met by the tea stall the previous morning. As he downed the hot, sweet tea, he sensed a penetrating stare by his side. Turning to find a middle-aged man with an overgrown moustache and slightly unkempt appearance on his right, Manu offered him a cup of tea. Accepting the offer, the two men sat on the bench in front of the tea stall comfortably sipping from their matkas (clay pots) and watching the busy street ahead of them. The man remarked casually that he was a holistic practitioner. Manu, though uninterested, let the man talk. He genuinely wanted a diversion. The gist of his long discourse was this:

Holistic practitioners are of the perception that the human body has the capacity to heal itself. One has to remain patient and stay attuned to nature and her synergies whereby the body's intimate messages could be perceived thereby spearheading the process of reversal. It is essential to forget what has been learnt so far. If the transition is meant to happen, it will. Whatever the outcome, one is required to stay calm, tuned in and breathe!

What sprung into Manu's mind as he lay on his bed was amazement at the sudden appearance of the man that morning. Perhaps he was a regular perhaps not. Whatever it was, the essence of his talk offered fresh perspective into dimensions that constituted the human body. This was an aspect of science that required deeper observation. Perhaps the man had noticed the look of utter desolation on Manu's face and pitied him enough to offer some semblance of hope? The thought however, offered him no consolation at all.

*

The short stop at Sanji Chhat near Ardhkuari offered a well-deserved rest. From here emerged two routes one of which continued as the pony trail. Breathing in air that smelled fresh as opposed to the earlier smellier route what with the animals freely littering the path with their dung, urine and snorts, Manav continued his walk at the unhurried pace he had set for himself. Another two and-a-half kilometer to go before the collective group of buildings called as 'the Bhawan' besides the temple was reached.

'March along, Mr. Fancy pants sans the footwear. You rock the look!' Whispery laughter rose and ebbed, accompanied by the gentle chants of pilgrims that passed him by.

He had heard about the holy shrine and its three-faced rock formation of the Mother Goddess that remained submerged at times within the holy cave. There were no idols or pictures of deities and Manav was prepared to wait in the queue for as long as it took just to have a glimpse of the one who had called. He knew that his request had been heard. All he wanted was for it to be granted. He would neither chant nor fold his hands in supplication. He had travelled a long way to meet the Mata. Prostrating before her for the sake of doing so seemed abhorrent to him. Baring one's heart and soul to the divine was what he believed in. She knew his inherent traits and he felt exposed. Bleeding and raw he was and he would not move from the vicinity until he was sure. She had brought him here all the way from the south and he would shift only when he was asked to make the call. There was no reason for him to continue. Why should he, when his existence depended on the one reason that had sustained him for this long? Manav was adamant. He would sleep outdoors, give up all amenities but he needed to hear the reply that he had come here for. His Maariyamman had to answer to him. After all, the Wise one had seen her for what she really was.

The Koteeswari in their midst was, in fact, a reflection of the love that had been acquired in exchange for pure, selfless service. Granted, his Sagu was financially stable. The stability was of the unbridled kind, endless like the waves in the ocean. But it was what she gave away that created multifold happiness.

One word, several dimensions. The Wise One had been far sighted.

Therefore, he – Manavlal Yadav would witness the rise of the Koteeswari this time around. There was no doubt on that. The beacon would rise, just as it should and train its light on all.

*

A Roundup of the Years

[*Gleaned through periodic online chats*]

Thanks to advances in technology and the milestones achieved in the field of communication by leaps and bounds, Core Z was able to recreate the missing aspects of each other's lives through intermittent chatting. Their group was named the same – Zenana. That would remain unchanged and password protected so that the kids, especially the curious ones, would not have access to information that was private and extremely confidential. The language was crude, downright vulgar at times, but that was a given considering the nature of relationship that the friends had. It helped them alleviate their stress and revive the old camaraderie. Precious memories that had dropped root in Oothukudi and branched out to lives recreated and enlivened by embracing new extensions. It felt as though each had grown feelers that gently extended, enquired and processed the wholesome change. Assimilating the newness seemed raw and open, allowing the senses to ascertain the depth of the extended phase. Every stage was explored and dissected in its minuteness and whatever the emotion felt, a limb was always there in more ways than one, to gather and garner support. The group thus formed a systemic interphase of thoughts, emotions, bonding and malleability that developed into a safety net of sorts. Sagu however, retained a meager part of her essence in comparison to the others. The realization dawned on the others at a rather delayed stage to effectively consider a rescue.

The chronicles below are a personalized version of the lives of the three friends during the interphase of the Zenana's separation, in an encapsulated form. This time again, the narration provides an insightful description about the highs and lows that abounded over the course of twenty-seven years for each of the Core Z member.

RATNA

Ratnalakshmi had offered to break the ice. The initial hesitation was obvious and the struggle to begin was evident to the others. However, once the reticence had been crossed, the words flowed unabated. The others read on without interruption.

'A lot of water has flowed under the bridge. I have changed and so have all of you. We are all the same age, four decades and more... That is the only similarity we share today. That, and an uncommon heritage in the form of Oothukudi and some wonderful school years spent at the Silver Flower HSS. The salve to my wounds had appeared and reappeared in many forms and that made me a wholesome person ably managing life and its vagaries without any form of blinkers being worn.

I was a reluctant bride. Sagu's wedding and the meeting with all of you along with your families made me understand that I was ready. Ready for discussions and exchange of personal experiences. The time for sharing has come. A solemn occasion such as this does not warrant for expressions of puzzlement, consternation and, riotous laughter. That would happen for sure once my story is unraveled. As for the real me, I am what I am now solely because of Raj.

He completed me. Made me whole.

Helped me see and feel the light.

Gave me Sanchita. Her coming transformed me, blossomed into my being, beyond my wildest dreams. I am now aware- aware of the depth and beauty of life. There had been instances in my childhood- that you know, which had terrorized me and taken me through periods of darkness. But the advent of Raj changed all of that. Raj was different.

I first met him at a typing center in my second year of college. I was working as an intern at a nearby pharmacy for a month and compilation of the weekly notes meant delivering them in a typed format to our lecturer. In those days, typing on our own via the desktop was not the norm. After instructing the typist on how the sheaf of handwritten notes were to be transcribed and the format to be followed, I walked up to the counter to pay the required fee and there he was; an unassuming slight young man with nut brown skin and a serious manner. Taken aback, I enquired about the regular guy who owned-cum-manned the center, and he answered that he was helping his friend (the regular guy), since he had to be someplace that day. We exchanged pleasantries and I discovered that he was a mechanical engineer who had just started working but had taken off on that particular day., as he seemed to have developed a bad cough and symptoms of malaria. This caught me off-guard. Malaria and cough?? That didn't match. I was a student of microbiology and reasoning suggested that this was total fabrication. Apparently, our pal wanted some time off or was toying with me! I pretended nonchalance, nodded and ambled away.

Mr. Malaria was present the next day when I went to collect my papers and he smiled sheepishly at me. His friend at the counter remarked that I was quite sharp and that he should have thought twice before fabricating such outlandish statements. The three of us laughed heartily at that and Raj mentioned that he had quit his present job and was travelling to Hyderabad the same week to join a bigger organization. His family was against his decision and wanted him to stay and manage one of their convenience stores. They had a few stores scattered around town but the only son and heir wanted a life that was disconnected from his roots. No sitting and counting out coins for provisions sold to households for him. He would carve out a different path for himself and make his family proud. Wishing him luck, I walked back to the college campus. I hoped that his dreams were realized. I knew that dreams were important especially for someone who was single, and struggling to stay afloat. I wondered how it would feel... having to rebel against a family who cared for you and always ensured that your wallet was always full of cash. Apparently, he was doted upon and his two elder sisters treated him with devotion akin to piety. It seemed pretty revolting to me and perhaps that was why he was doing a turnaround. The claustrophobia tends to hit on you one way or another.

My postgraduate studies took back me to Ooty after a year. This time I chose to stay with my second sister and needless to say, she was ecstatic. My life revolved around college, the postgraduate course in Biotechnology and my sisters of course. I felt relief wash over me at not having to pick at foods that were tasteless and most often, way past the expiry date. I enjoyed being pampered by my siblings who visited me once too often. It was an enjoyable time for us altogether. In deference to my wishes, not a word was mentioned with regard to the man who had fathered us. To me, he was all but dead and anyone who wished to renew the relationship with the man, was off-limits too. My brother-in-law indulged me as well. Of course, owing to my monthly allowance my financial needs were adequately taken care of and did not put a strain on their resources. The cynical self within me however, constantly echoed that this was the cause of my being tolerated at home. Whatever the reason, everyone seemed to be happy. Perhaps my brother-in-law was genuinely good at heart; I did not know and did not wish to conjecture on that. After my school days, the next best time I had experienced, was at my sister's home in Ooty.

It was on one particularly wintry day as I approached the gates of the college that I noticed a shivering figure huddled beneath an inadequate shawl besides the amused gatekeeper.

One might wonder how I had zeroed in upon this figure when there were several others loitering around aimlessly, with some sipping piping hot tea from plastic cups or, the purposeful ones aiming to target their beau.

The trick was in the clothes. Wearing two layers of thermal innerwear beneath my woolen ensemble enabled me to continue ambling with a purposeful gait. No fool unless mad, would drape himself in a threadbare shawl and wait in weather that was designed to freeze your bones. Unless this was a dare or, a person unaccustomed to the weather or, a man in love, the last choice I seriously doubted, it had to be the second reason. Narrowing down the choices, I further reasoned that this had to be someone who had never been exposed to subzero temperatures. This accounted for the figure vibrating in utter helplessness (similar to a prong was my dispassionate observation) and well, he seemed to be turning blue in the face too. Imagine my shock when a close scrutiny revealed the identity of the person as being none other than Mr. Malaria! Our man seemed ready to pass out and so, I found myself towing him into the kitchen area of the canteen with the gatekeeper's help since the place was considerably warmer.

It took the best part of an hour for him to be revived what with my classes for the day having to be skipped and a good part of my daily allowance that I kept a strict watch on, being spent to boost the body temperature of someone I barely knew. I curbed my annoyance by reminding myself that helping someone who was in need was the moral duty of a non-practicing Hindu as well. After being bundled in warmer 'uppers and lowers' donated by kind members of the canteen management, Mr. Malaria was finally ready to talk.

It appeared that he had spent two fruitful years in Hyderabad successfully negotiating the 'ladder of fame and fortune' when he had received the telegram from his parents. His grandmother was on her deathbed and wished to see her grandson and last surviving heir before she departed to the nether world. Rushing to Trichy, Raj was able to wish his grandmother one last goodbye and accede to her dying wish which was to chuck the city life and manage the inheritance that his parents had so painstakingly built for him. Raj was now the Managing Director of M/s Pathy's chain of stores that stocked everything from nails to condoms within its old-fashioned precincts. Let me tell you that I had not laughed as much that day as I did in years. And what of the grandmother-on-the-deathbed? Raj's ears had turned a bright red. She had recovered and was inching albeit hobblingly towards the ripe old age of ninety-two.

So...why was he here? Dare I ask him? It was not anything to do with the college, of that I was sure. My mind reasoned out the explanation. My first choice was obviously wrong. But there was no sane explanation other than the one my mind had latched onto. The tops of his ears turned an even brighter red. And, this is how the rest of our short conversation went:

Raj: "Well, as you know, I have always been thinking about you. And Cookie (the typing center owner, our mutual friend) had kept me informed of your whereabouts. He advised me to tread with caution. At present though, I'm done with caution. My life is at stake."

Me: "Are you off your head? The cold has addled your brain I think. What the hell are you trying to say? I seriously do not have the time for this."

Raj: "Look, don't get me wrong. Everything's moving too fast for you, I know...."

Me: "Mr. Malaria - that has to be the understatement of the day! Apart from your weird behavior, that is."

Raj: "Lakshmi, I like you a lot but could never pipe up the courage to strike up a decent conversation with you even then. I've had your phone number with me by the way. But what set my tail on fire is that my lovely grandmother and even lovelier parents plus the sisters and troupe are conspiring to get me married. Well, what do you know, I have informed them that I've been engaged to you since about a year and that we are planning to get hitched as soon as your course gets over next year!"

You can imagine my embarrassment what with several eager sets of ears ready to run off and relay the latest romantic misadventure happening within its fair walls. I was flummoxed and wished that a sinkhole would swallow me right that instant. Mr. Malaria had the cheek to talk his way through an audacious scheme with good old me as partner. How did I end up in the grand scheme of things was way beyond my powers of perception. The whole idea in its absurdity required courage that only someone like Raj could dream of.

Leaving his family in chaos, Raj had fled without a change of clothes to accost me and keep me in the loop. The family members were in the throes of the wildest speculation about the girl, her background, her financial position, etc. Watching the hopeful expression on the man's face bought a smile to my face. This had to be the biggest real-life comical situation I have ever faced. The fictional girlfriend, who also happened to be physically challenged, was supposed to save her desperate boyfriend from the web of bondage.

We found ourselves laughing in sheer mirth. I, who had never dreamt of a relationship, my physical disability being the perfect impediment, was now being pursued in the most ridiculous manner and was actually considering the trappings that went with it. My sisters would be over the moon of course but the thought of interacting with his family gave me the chills.

And so after a year, I came to be known as Raj's wife. He had to undertake several trips to convince me of his sincerity. To save his skin, I had agreed to pose as his 'loving girlfriend' but after a while, it set my teeth on edge. I was threatened in various ways; through phone calls, men posing as well-wishers hinting at physical harm, oblique remarks that demeaned me as an individual, my physical frailty as a hindrance towards child bearing and so on. Never did any of these taunts or jibes upset me. On the contrary, it made me admire the man who dared take up the challenge and throw caution to the winds. It made me appreciate his generous nature and loving heart. Despite having all that one could wish for, he chose me to spend the rest of his life with. And that was beyond the spirit of generosity. This was love that the man had for me. The emotion that made him take a stand against the bigots within his family.

Raj relinquished his legacy and started a small grocery store in Chennai with his meager savings. Our daughter was born in the year 2000. I joined the Biotech campus at Tambaram as a junior professor. After passing the UGC qualifiers, I moved up to being an assistant professor at the Pollachi Government College earning a decent pay and living a simple and fulfilled life. I have since learned to cook chicken biryani like a pro and can manage the household quite well. If you consider the earlier version of Ratna, whose inability to differentiate between a ladle and spoon was a running joke amongst all, my accomplishments thus far, have been a major achievement.

My disability of the physical kind will serve as a reminder that despite everything life throws at us, the essence of true happiness lies within us. The gift of the olive branch that is extended has to be recognized, grabbed and, utilized to its fullest before it fades from view. The olive branch I came across that cold day in the form of Raj was life giving me the very best that it could offer. And, that, my friends, is the story of Lakshmi's life in a nutshell.'

*

MARGE XAVIER

Graduating out of high school with decent marks was quite an achievement for Marge who had relied on Sagu to get by since the time they had met. She barely managed to get through the first year of college, weighed in as she was by thoughts of her dearest friend, Sagu. Tragedy struck the second time over with the passing away of her ailing mother. Marge and her father slowly grew to rely upon each other unlike the father-daughter duo normally seen in traditional Indian communities. With the absence of a motherly figure, there was an easy camaraderie shared between the two and household chores coupled with official duties were tackled fairly well. Their neighbors often remarked upon the ease with which the daughter rode her father's Royal Enfield motorbike all around town with the father ensconced; pillion mode behind her. Weekends would be spent with the daughter efficiently working and cleaning the heavy two-wheeler, changing its spark plug, repairing punctures, changing tires, etc. with hands that were stained dark with grease. The father was always seen reprimanding and directing the girl. Marge soon struck a friendship with a local vehicle repair center and visited the site quite often to obtain tips and favors. The girl whizzed around town with two or three of her classmates perched excitedly behind her and teamed up with local boys who were part of the regular motorcycle pack. Long biking trips took a toll on studies and the father-daughter duo decided to shift from active college education to a correspondence (postal) course to allow increased leeway towards her passion. Online courses were a rarity in those days and this route offered the girl a chance to focus on something that she was passionate about. You might remember the stock market option that we had read about earlier that Marge had wanted to pursue. However, what came about after detailed discussions with her father was that, Marge would pursue a year or two, of working in Peter's vehicle repair center, provided he agreed to the unusual arrangement and then, think of taking the next step forward.

A perceptive Sagu had interrupted her with the question, "What initiated the shift in interest towards vehicles, Margie?" A slight knowing smile followed the remark. "It couldn't have been a random reason. There had been some kind of a trigger. What set you off?"

Marge had acknowledged her bestie's perceptive query with an answering laugh. She had replied, "You are absolutely right, Sagu. It was a supremely masochistic reaction by a few members of the opposite sex that got to me and proved to be the turning point. Let me tell you all what actually happened."

'There were three of us riding our motorbikes along the outskirts of the town on a hot afternoon. I had Mahesh behind me and there was Sam riding his Suzuki with girlfriend Sheila. Then there was macho Raghu or, 'Raks' as he liked to be called with his stooges- the Double D's; Dilip and Daniel squashed behind him on his Honda.' I was jeered at by most boys for daring to ride a vehicle solely designed for men but the admiring glances of the girls gave me the courage to continue and of course, my father's encourage-ment kept me going. Mahesh was a sweet boy and he often piped up in my defense although members of his tribe often sadly outnumbered him. Which was why he agreed to be my riding partner that day and our vehicles growled and zoomed through the hard, unbaked dusty roads towards a village that Raks said he was familiar with. I was riding my father's Bullet that looked pretty impressive which was why I was allowed into the haloed portals of Raks bike squad. I secretly thanked my wonderful father for allowing me to handle his bike and teaching me to ride it. Bullet owners are notoriously possessive and to override that feeling and teach a slip of a girl who also happens to be the darling daughter, rev up and take charge of the petrol-guzzling monster, was a feat by itself. I was pretty sure that had Deenanna been with us, I would be attending classes during the day and returning home after that to cook and manage our home. I was blessed to have my father's guidance throughout. It didn't matter to us that the aunties of my neighborhood and the so-called 'respected members of the society' disapproved of our actions. I was the poster child for the 'anti-girl behavior' brigade those days and in the following days to come I would reinforce that phrase with a vengeance.

The motorcycle hummed smoothly with rhythmic precision as I followed the two bikes ahead of me. I felt the hot breeze on my arms and face and smiled happily. This seemed to be the best day of my life. I pictured my classmates scribbling notes as the lecturer droned on. It was a relief to be away from the claustrophobic confines of the classroom. If only my friends knew the kind of freedom we were experiencing at this moment, how they would envy us yet not have the nerve to follow what was being practiced. I detested forced pedagogy. There was no fun in it. Sagu had been the one who had helped me endure the boredom. With her by my side, I turned passive and joyful. Together, we painted our world in the brightest of colors and watched it bloom.

My reverie was interrupted by a loud 'twang' soon after which, we jerked to a stop. I flicked the stand down with my foot and bent down on my haunches to inspect the vehicle. There was a thin trail of oil that was dripping down from someplace but I had no clue as to what had happened to the bike. After several ineffectual kicks to get the bike going, I finally stopped, heaving with exertion. Mahesh was noticeably upset. Being stranded with the 'girl-who-was-a-rebel,' away from town under the sweltering sun was an unattractive prospect. I scanned the horizon for my teammates. They were long gone and only a fine cloud of dust trailed behind them and that too, seemed to be gradually dissipating. Annoyed at my ignorance and bad luck, I suggested that we walk and try to find a garage that could set things right. Mahesh agreed grudgingly and we trudged slowly, following the trail that our friends had left behind them. Mahesh did not offer to help and neither did it cross my mind to ask as I pushed and walked alongside the bike.

After what seemed to be a long time, we could see the two bikes of our companions coming towards us. We were greeted with hoots and cheers. Raks jeered and exclaimed with his customary sneer, "So… the golden girl is in trouble and, does not know what is wrong with her beauty bike." Guffaws followed. I knew that the bike I rode was the subject of envy and it had pleased me until a while earlier. Sam and Sheila were grinning broadly. The 'Double D's' continued in the same vein, voices dripping with sarcasm. "Don't think that this trip will include golden girl anymore, Raks. It's time for you (indicating me) to turn back and put an end to the grand dream."

The feeling of devastation, of being left out in the lurch had been heartbreaking. For a moment it had felt good to be a part of something that was never there. It had all been a delusion. Misconstrued reality that was tangible yet, unreal.

Weary and dizzy from the effort of trudging several kilometers with an extra heavy bike didn't help boost an already depleting self-esteem level. Watching Mahesh suppress his grin and Sheila simper along with the boys made her realize the futility of trying to 'fit in'. Marge realized the importance of doing away with certain misconceptions in that one instant. Misconceptions created by society, the unwritten code that conveys the fact that girls are essentially weaker than men. She would fight the imbalance with every breath that she had and she, for one, would not kowtow to bullies such as these. Come what may, she would work on retribution. But, that would be something that everyone would appreciate and grudgingly respect.

So she straightened her back and looked at Mahesh and asked him to hop on Sam's bike. As he hesitated, Raks gestured to him and the threesome clung on the two bikes. Her nod indicated that they continued their journey and she would go back and do what she needed to do.

*

Marge created a buzz in the neighborhood those days. It was sad; friends and relatives remarked with aspersion that the father was seen acceding to his daughter's unusual wish. Had the mother been alive, she would have probably gotten married and sent off to live with her in-laws. This was abnormal. A girl working in full view of everyone that too, with vehicles of all shapes and sizes and, interacting with men was unacceptable according to esteemed members of the society. Nothing unfazed Mr. Xavier though. He turned a deaf ear towards the naysayers and assumed that his daughter would be treated with kindness at the workshop. Her age and fondness for the machines would be given due consideration was his conjecture. The erroneous assumption led him to request Peter to take her on as an apprentice. He knew that she would be at her happiest tinkering with machines and learning what she could from them. The request was an unusual one but Peter agreed to the suggestion without hesitation.

The vehicle repair center had been set up by Peter's father who had hoped to see his son do justice to the ambitious venture. However, Peter proved to be simplistic in outlook and lacked the drive towards conversion of opportunities that came his way. This was further acerbated by the lackadaisical attitude of his employees who were associated with the center since its inception.

Starting with two-wheelers Marge was made a junior apprentice to the dismay of her co-workers and that meant taking up the tireless, often, thankless job of repairing lowly bicycles, scooters and motorcycles. The girl's passion was evident. Neither the sun, winds or cloudy skies deterred her from reaching her workplace on time. She reached early, pestered the men for help and suggestions, worked diligently and left late in the evening only after the father came around enquiring for her.

Initially, Marge's friends poked fun at her and the local boys shunned the services of the garage. Business was dull and this in turn, added to the resentment of her colleagues. They were paid a nominal monthly amount, which they feared would disappear if the customers avoided visiting their center. Marge herself had cuts, nicks, smelly clothes and bad hair days though her cheerful demeanor cut through all of her troubles and exhaustion. To avoid reacting to frosty behavior was part of her training as well. It was evident that except for Peter and her father who saw through her sincerity and allowed her to persevere, all the others waited to see the day when the girl would stumble and fail. It would be good to see her walk away. They were just about done with the circus.

At home, a washed up and clean Marge would update her manual; jotting down all that she had seen and learnt during the day. Titled 'Marge's Mini Manual,' the initial entry began with her favorite vehicle, the Royal Enfield Bullet. A rough sketch of the motorcycle in the first page followed by pointers on various Brands and their kinds, market price, components: main body, assembly: melding of the parts, types of damage and the possible causes, repair, location of spare parts and, overall service were recorded. The book thus provided a comprehensive overview into the world of mechanical moving machines and later proved to be a commercial must-have among interns who jostled at the bit, eager to use the guide as a tool to help further their aim. The entries were crisp and to the point. Some pages had ink stains and grease marks on them. A few pointers were crossed out while others were rewritten. There were several short entries noted on the left hand side of the page, alongside the margin. The short scribbles were easy to understand and written using simple layman terms. As Marge's understanding and experience grew, so did her notes, ready references and quick tips that helped garner instant results. What Marge had begun as a self-help tool, proved to be an instant guide that was recommended for use at homes along with the Yellow Pages and much later, as an ancillary textbook for students as part of the engineering syllabi. The Mini manual had created a mini revolution of sorts.

[Inset: A leaf out of the original copybook has been reprinted for the reader's reference.]

Marge's Mini Manual

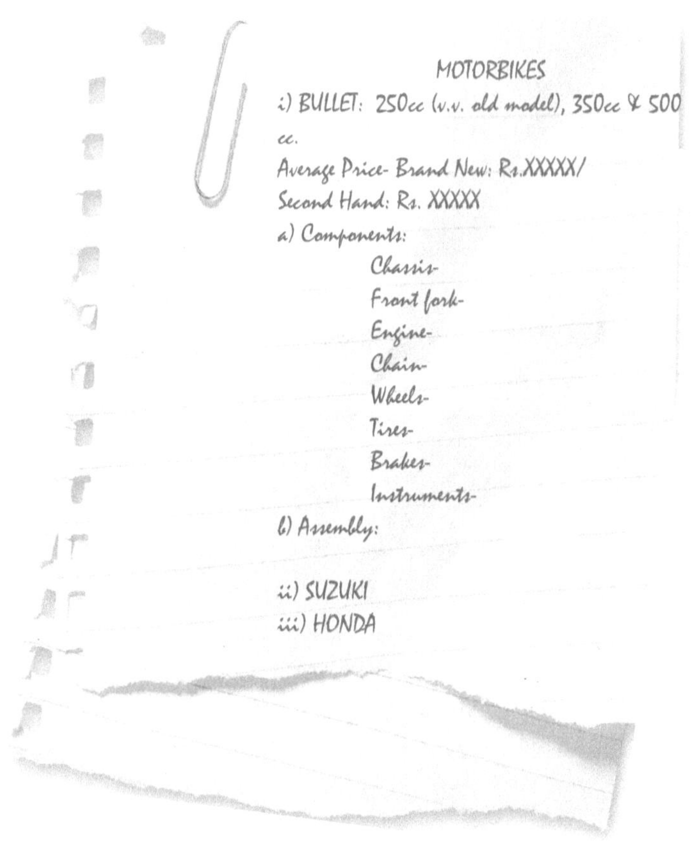

.... and so on.

Marge was paid a student allowance, which she offered to forego and divide by three to enable topping up of her co-workers' salaries. Peter eagerly accepted the offer as he too found the going difficult and promised to reimburse her once business picked up. Her irked colleagues Babu, John and, Antony remained unaware of this gesture. Their asperity increased as the girl began moving up the level to begin her apprenticeship on four-wheelers and they now considered quitting the center. The prospect was an uphill task as they were not getting any younger. Worry settled upon them like a cloud as they had grown to think of the workplace as their second home. Peter was a kind and considerate employer and they had most of the vehicular services centered on their little enterprise. A dwindling income was one among several issues they had to contend with and to move to the city to look for alternate arrangements frankly worried them.

On site, the girl was offered no privacy and had to share the same wash-cum-restroom that was used by the male members. Jokes and humor stilled when she neared the vicinity. Often Marge would return home teary-eyed and humiliated. It has to be noted here that, had her father not provided unstinting support and encouragement, Marge would have given up on her passion without hesitation. Also with fierce Deenanna out of the way, the father-daughter duo was free to live their lives in the manner that they thought fit.

Once Marge decided to take a day off to meet her college mates. It was a sudden decision. The idea was to convince them to visit the garage and avail their services since they offered the best rates in the area. The so-called offer was a desperate gamble. Marge knew that she was offering a lot for something she had no control over but she needed the men around her. She needed to stay in the garage. Books were never meant to be, in her case. She had found the love of her life and for that to remain on its feet, she had to trust her instincts. Her only prayer was that she would be taken seriously.

Babu, John and, Antony on the other hand, seized the opportunity to confront Peter. The idea was to convince him of the necessity in sending away the young upstart. A novel idea such as this was proving to be a detriment and only young, eligible men came up to have their vehicles serviced while they checked out the girl and cooked up petty favors. It was beneath them to watch such goings-on when business was not doing really well. Peter had noticed the simmering tension and resentment amongst his male workers for quite a while although the girl had never mentioned anything of importance to him. Barring the girl's voluntary distribution of her allowance towards the three, never, for once had she spoken of any issue that disturbed or upset her. Peter was secretly impressed by her courage and resilience. Her dedication and commitment towards the craft of her choice was a heroic feat. Gently admonishing the men for failing to see the good in the girl who was also indirectly supporting their families (in a minor way) and continuing to follow the same male oriented thinking that forced women within the four walls of their homes, Peter said that he supported Marge totally and that they were free to leave if they wanted to do so. For him, it was the quality of work and the eagerness to deliver that mattered not, petty politics.

The three men were suitably chastened and quiet, mulling over Peter's words over cups of tea when sounds of vehicles churning up the driveway echoed through the thin walls of the garage. Rushing out, they watched a bevy of two-wheelers enter the compound and park within the premises. It was Marge, who had brought along her friends to check out the workshop that she was interning in. The curious students admired the girl and her tenacity and mentioned as much. The three men were vociferous in their agreement to Marge's surprise and proceeded to show them around. Peter discussed the rates for the services offered and announced a 20% discount on the total bill for all the students and their friends.

The 'Bullet Girl' had thus, officially come into being. Marge was gifted a second hand Royal Enfield Bullet after the stupendous closing of sales for the second month in succession. Peter was glad that his instincts did not fail him. Desertion of three of his best employees would have meant that the garage be closed down. It was an off-the-cuff decision he had made when challenged. But the move had worked in his favor and he was glad about the outcome. The girl, he had to admit was good. She was good with all vehicles but the two-wheelers, those were her specialty. How she managed to write and clear her second and third year exams were a mystery but no one cared about that anyway. Besides having the college kids and staff over at his garage at all times, there were people from around the city and far-flung areas who travelled with their vehicles just to have it set right by the Bullet Girl. Marge was quoted as an example and her dedication for the craft was highlighted. She became the toast of her co-workers and her neighbors swore by her name when they picked on their children. Many college dropouts stopped by the workshop to enquire for vacancies and work under her as interns but, she referred them to Babu, John and, Antony in deference to their age and experience. The three men in turn, taught the girl all that they knew and pestered Peter to construct a separate washroom with a tiny cubicle for her. This, for her was true recognition!

In time, Marge's father helped her start her first workshop in the city. It was named Peter's Auto service center in honor of her mentor. An overwhelmed Peter offered to handover the garage he had built from scratch to Marge while retaining a share of the profits and she gladly accepted. He retired from the field, easy at heart and happy in the belief that his enterprise would continue to flourish. It was providence that had brought Marge to him and what a legacy the girl was continuing to create! Babu, John and

Antony were elevated to Managerial positions and they had a team of fine young men and women to help with the sales and after service jobs. Most of the apprentices who had interned with them at the original center were retained by Marge and together; they handled the running of the new workshops admirably well.

The time was right for the town's favorite girl to get hitched. Soon, the father of the local church sent word that a suitable boy had been found and indeed, by God's Grace, he was a fine young man. True to his nature, the groom demonstrated complete acceptance and supported his wife's unusual work ethos. Thus, Marge Xavier was married off to Packiam Samuel and was henceforth known as Mrs. Marge 'Bullet' Packiam.

*

For five years, the couple remained childless. Marge was a busy woman and with Packiam receiving an overseas job offer that included a year of study, the odds were closing in. It was mutually decided that he would fly to Orlando and complete his course and return. Frequent calls notwithstanding, it took a year and a half for him to return and savor life once again with his successful wife. Marge's father was gradually turning frail and the couple insisted that he move in with them. When official duties upped the pressure forcing Packiam to consider yet another offer that would take him to where he had been placed earlier, Marge saw red and put down her foot. It was high time that they started planning for a family but it didn't seem likely that Marge would ever throw away what she had painstakingly built after all the struggle over the years. Kids were but a natural step towards the progression of a family and as such, five years had flown away without either of them realizing the fact. Before the ladies of the community read her the riot act, they'd better show some progress after which she assured him, he was free to take up whatever offers came his way.

And so, the trials and tribulations began. Guided by an able gynecologist, Martha and Packiam stepped into the emerging world of parenthood. Their initial efforts were a disaster and Marge suffered two consecutive miscarriages. The two felt haunted and avoided family parties and social occasions. Marge began to feel inadequate for the first time in her life. The working nature of all things moving and mechanical, she knew but, the one thing she was concerned about right then, was something she was unaware of and Marge began to feel the lack of a maternal figure at home. She realized that she had been selfish and should have encouraged her father to remarry. Perhaps a lady in the house would have helped them look things through a different viewpoint. It would have made her father content and given her, someone to open up and share matters related to all things feminine.. Had Marge known that her bestie could have lent her a helping hand, her relief would have been paramount but fate works in mysterious ways. Situations that warrant action could turn the other way. Nothing is by chance. Everything is appropriate and rooted in the moment.

Frustrated and feeling poorly, Marge was advised to try something unheard of in their part of town. It was called the IVF treatment and was available in Chennai at a reputed hospital. Marge and Packiam were advised to try their luck since dearth of money was not a deterrent towards achievement of something this personal. Following several visits, Marge finally conceived and the couple was blessed with twin boys. The confinement, total bed rest and physical exertion had drained the new mother but their family was now complete. The baptism ceremony of Arul and Andrew Packiam was a lavish affair followed by celebrations within the household and Madam Marge's workforce. A nanny and cook were hired to cope with the rising volume of work within the household. Marge cut down her work schedule to thrice-a-week work-from-home days. The room at the back of her home was converted to an office with phone and fax lines manned by an efficient secretary along with a custom state-of-the-art desktop that kept track of her business, a system unheard of in those days. Packiam was finally allowed to choose the job of his liking and travel as he fancied provided, he was home during the weekends. Their children would grow up having their parents interact and bask in the pleasures of their little world. Single parenting had its benefits. She was what she was, thanks to her doting father but the lack of a mother when it really mattered, left an impact regardless of age and maturity. For Arul and Andrew, Mummy and Daddy would always be around to watch them grow and develop for as long as they were meant to remain on this good earth. If it was God's will that they stay long enough to enjoy and watch the fruit of their actions, it would be the greatest of blessings bestowed on each one of them.

*

SHRUTHI

'My life has remained pretty normal unlike my friends who have had amazing twists and turns in their chequered little lives. The everyday routine that I follow is an inexhaustible yet, predictable pattern that leave little time for introspection. Tasks that might seem mundane from the outside are the very pivots around which, the ethereal orchestration of time (within my household) tunes into. Just as cells are considered the basis of all living organisms, so are we, the unknown; duty bound homemakers, queens of our individual nuclear kingdoms.

It's important for me to let you all know that you should not lose your sense of self-esteem at any cost. The fact remains that when you feel low, you feel like those scrunched up pieces of paper that has been casually tossed into the waste bin. You cannot uncrumple yourself and begin from where you had initially started. There are moments when you are reduced to levels beyond comprehension that only the mundane tasks help in keeping sanity intact. You end up consoling yourself by saying that there are too many of us around. So why am I the only one complaining? The choice was mine, wasn't it? Why the heck didn't I opt for that ophthalmology course for heaven's sake? I have berated myself, treated my inner self with scorn, desisted from flinging away everything I have ever loved and have finally, ceased to ponder over the unwelcome thoughts.

For argument's sake, it can be said that none can measure up to the organizational levels we have achieved when faced with the herculean task of managing a home rather efficiently. To loosely give you an example of how Shruthi *mami's*[32] (I am fondly known by this name here, at Oothukudi) precious seconds could be accounted for; picture the kids and hubby out of the way and the round of morning chores being cleared from the checklist. Perhaps I would have dozed off for half an hour, which is rare unless I happen to be extremely indisposed and trawling about the bed in delusion. The day being a working Saturday and a half day at that, the trio would be reaching home in two hours' time, so, I would probably go about things in this way…

Look at the clock. Stifle a scream. Hear the constant tinkle of the messages piling up on the phone. No time to check them however, and groan out loud.

Shift to HiSpeed mode—Begin Routine #n^1 (n to the power of 1).

- Sort clothes. Add softener and detergent. Get the machine running.
- Clear containers. Stock all extras in the freezer. Wash vessels. Scrub, Scour. Run the tap. Rinse, Stack. Rinse, Stack.
- Wipe countertop. Oven top. Run the scrub cloth over countertop tiles. Clean those oil spots. There. Done.
- Zero time to sweep and mop. Hose up and Vacuum. Power clean and dust everything in sight.
- Check messages. Husband plus friend coming over for a quick bite? Red alert!!!
- Look through contents of the fridge and kitchen cabinets. Sort, assemble, shred, chop, and season. Rapid-fire on those motions, lady.

The SUPER reflexes-cum-eye on the clock routine now comes into play. Bring out the homemade *athirasam*[26] jar- a Shruthi mami specialty. Time to show off the gooseberry pickle dedicated for just 'that' occasion.

- Beep alert - Shift to Routine #n^2. Take out clothes, ruffle, and hang to dry.
- Next, walk through rooms. Clean floors. Check.
- Toss those extra wipes away. Stuff stray pieces of clothing into the cupboard.
- Check bathroom. Inspect face. Smile.
- Check teeth. Smile. Purrrfect!

Wait for the doorbell to ring. Tick-tock-tick-tock. Husband dearest with the friend or, the brat pack? Either way, are we super-charged-ready for the upcoming session?! You bet.

Post lunch, hubby dearest and friend amble out for a quiet chat. Sri Ram works in the Postal division of the Indian Railways. It is a nine-to-five job; fairly sedate and stress-free. The brats are in high school, soon to enter college. I worry needlessly about the college fee, lack of medical insurance and, forthcoming marriage expenses for our daughter. My Sri Rama is basically laidback and keeps assuring me that the Good Lord will provide. Hrmpf! I do not want to argue needlessly. The topic continues to be a bone of contention between us.

My TV serials beckon. Two hours of oblivion during which time, the reactivation mode will be enabled.

I rifle through the remains of the afternoon lunch. Thinking of the extra servings stacked up in the freezer thrills me to bits. I'm not your regular *pattumami*[33] my dears. Dinner's taken care of through and through.

It's been a long wait. What's with the good husband? No calls so far. Should I do the honors? Or do I message? Hope it's not another late night. At my behest, he takes up freelance accounting jobs at a friend's tailoring shop. The extra bucks that come by, goes into my special kitty, my saving scheme for times of exigencies. I refuse to feel guilty for having pushed him into that. It's not a call-center kind of job he's in, for heaven's sake.

Just remembered the altered clothes at the tailors. Got to pick them up today. Rush and drop the brats for their evening class before the clothes are collected.

After breezing through that, spend an hour with another dear mami. We sip filter coffee from small tumblers and discuss the sitcom, the terrible weather, bills mounting up, expenses shooting through the roof and, of course, the next doubter—do we start work at a school? The conversation peters off. We lose interest. I am gently reminded of the time and duly rush out.

Pick up the kiddos, form our trio-kinship, manage the heated squabbles along the way, change and get ready for dinner and bedtime thereafter.

Plate up. Heat. Serve.

The kids gobble mirthfully while watching Rajini make short work of his adversaries and I listlessly pick on the eats. I'm drained and need to hit the bed for the four a.m. routine the next day. Lights are killed and I surrender to the exhaustion. Sunday mornings are reserved for temple visits. My timings are pretty static, you see. And that, my friends is pretty much how I get to spend my time.

*

Do you remember the one amazing time we had spent together on the terrace of our building? I watched the four of us excitedly plan a sleepover during one of my *shavaasan*[34] routine with such clarity. Upon realizing that the confines of our home had limitations with regard to space, on we trooped upstairs post dinner in all happiness. There were no fancy gadgets in our possession and neither was the ambience of the high-class sort. In our home back then, we did not have separate spaces where we could bury ourselves and do our thing.

I shared a room with my 'paatti' and she mumbled, snored and wheezed through most days and nights. Our house definitely looked threadbare from an outsider's point of view. We neither had fancy furniture nor clothes that reeked of modernity. Our lives followed a simple tradition namely, wake up early and complete an elaborate worship of the Gods after our victuals of course. Following this, we would begin our day's routine: Amma in the kitchen, school for me and, Appa to his den in the office. Paatti would continue with her chanting as she shouted out instructions by the dozen. Amma tolerated the belligerence while I loved her - loved the information stored inside of her head, that is. Oh, the tales of yore that she recounted, the lifestyle issues and her expertise in the culinary arts; that was what interested me the most! On the seven days that my mother was not allowed to enter the kitchen, I would sneak in and assist my father who churned out the same set menu every month. It would be rice-rasam-poriyal-appalam on one day and, rice-sambar-poriyal-appalam the next. I would help wash and cut the vegetables and offer to clean up as well. I didn't mind the work, as my relieved mother would allow me to remain awhile and try out items discussed with my paatti. It thus gave me quite a bit of confidence to create a sumptuous repast at the drop of a hat with very few ingredients thus supporting my passion over a formal career.

For the dinner prior to the sleep over, I went over the menu excitedly with my family. They suggested a simple meal as it would be easy on my hands and so it would be; vegetable semolina upma with stir fried baby potatoes, tiny sweet sesame flatcakes coated with jaggery and coconut stuffed dumplings that we would carry upstairs to savor while watching the star studded sky. Lying on our reed mats surrounded by whining mosquitoes and squinting through clouds of smoke let out by mosquito coils (there were eight of them) around us, we lay replete, our stomachs close to bursting. I was content since the unabashed admiration of the girls had made me glow with pride. Sagu had surprised us with a ready game of her own making. Calling it 'Remake at Random' we were to come out with a question that was the opposite of logic and reply along the same lines. The game would be developed as we progressed. Sagu would begin she said, just to make us understand.

Pointing to the sky she asked, "What if there were no shooting stars? Think of a star going back to wherever it came from."

There was a silence…of puzzlement. We were trying to figure out what that meant.

"Did anyone get it?" enquired Ratna awkwardly.

"Nope," countered Marge. "She comes up with bizarre ideas anyway."

"What I meant was, to think of something that is not regular. My answer to the question would be– to grant a wish instead of asking for one when we view a star-that-is-returning," concluded Sagu matter-of-factly.

"OK then, my turn. What would Deenanna do when not flexing his knuckles," asked Ratna amidst titters to which the sister promptly replied, "Not ride Daddy's Bullet?" There were hoots and barks of delight and the game caught on. We whispered into the night until slumber crept up on us. Sagu's intelligent one-liner runs through my mind every now and then.

'To grant a wish instead of asking for one.'

How very prophetic – and poetic! This was our girl doing exactly what she said, in the classic 'Sagu' way. She was fulfilling the wishes of several that came her way.

Coming back to the present, there is nothing much I can think of beyond my time-bound schedule that require my services apart from my home and family. Perhaps after my daughter is married and son settled in his career, I could think of broadening my horizons with respect to my 'famed' culinary skills. We might not have the necessary infrastructure or investment to begin something in a gigantic way but perhaps with Sri Ram's pension to help get by I could work on something from home. What do you think of the name Shruthi's Savories? I could prepare and deliver *murukkus*[27], athirasam, *thokkus*[88], *gongura chutney*[29], appalams and *vadagams*[30] from home. Sounds good doesn't it? Sagu and Margie could give me a tip or two on how to run my little outfit. I feel emboldened with them around; my wonderful friends who have achieved so much, despite the highs and lows. Core Z reloaded- with Dr. Sagarika Murthy Yadav, Lakshmi, Marge 'Bullet' Packiam and, yours truly a.k.a. Shruthi mami, do we pack quite the punch!

For now though, I am content.
I am fine.

*

Nik Beauty Parlour
SHRUTHI'S SAVORIES
SELVAM electronics

EPILOGUE

THE PALLIATIVE WARD (VIP ROOM #1)

I hate glum faces. When you are active and far busier than can ever be imagined, you generally tend to forget the feeling of what is happening inside of you. But having to watch 'that' look on others is something I tend to avoid. It disturbs and acts as a constant reminder. Acceptance is something one must cultivate. That imparts a serene feel.

Life has been kind to me. My temple is intact and running and I am in its precincts today, to test its merits. Ha Ha. So far… so good.

Murugan though, is one feisty soul. I did not ask for him to be here. But the steely look of determination on his face… that, I recognize.

Manu had left in a huff. I know his heart through and through. Never mind, achy heart. Doremi will see you in your revitalized avatar. Don't be too long though.

There are a few loose ends to be knotted and certain instructions that must be followed to the letter. I shall strive to keep up the perfection. Tiredness be damned! Need to keep the light shining for just a little while.

Of the lives I have touched and seen at close quarters, several wait outside to wish and bless me. Their numbers are increasing by the hour, I am told. Although forbidden, I gesticulate for the wheelchair. It is time for their Periyamma to return the love. With the sunshine on my face and a trembling Murugan by my side, I face the rousing cries of the crowd. Palpable emotions surround me as I fold my palms together and bow my head. I am calm and at peace. My heart flutters like a little bird heaving within its web of contentment. I thank nature for the wondrous life I've had. This life.

A smiling image flash before my eyes. It was of the Wise One. I smile back at him and murmur, "I had it figured, O blissful Guru. You were right."

*

An excerpt from the red autograph book (year 1986) preceded by a brief foreword from Dr. Sagarika (Murthy) Yadav.

I chanced upon this worn treasure among the assorted collection of books that are now being compiled and boxed into cartons for donation to various libraries across the city. The childish scrawls within amused me. One, in particular caught my fancy.

Roses are red and violets are blue,
But my heart will always be with you

- Joyonto/Grade VI

Cheesy but sweet. Another gem went this way:

Shining star, do be brave
For you, this friend shall always pray

- Manjari (Monjudi), best friend & neighbor

We were leaving Assam and notes of dejection had occupied most of the little pages. I had felt ragged with misery on the last day of school. Little was I to know that soon, lasting bonds of comradeship would chance upon me and offer comfort; embracing me within their soothing folds.

As I flipped through, it was evident that the Marvel heroes and associated characters that I was obsessed with, had lent my imagination wings. These took the form of tightly squeezed, sometimes illegible notes that were penned in the final pages of the book. Making sense of the misspelt words and grammatical errors, I have attempted to recreate the same in as comprehensible a manner as possible. I wish I had remembered the outline of the plot to enrapture Chandru during the few bedtime sessions we had shared during his childhood. The narrative would have kept him engrossed for sure.

I hope that you (dear reader) do not look at this offering with a jaundiced eye rather, think of the girl who had dreams of being at one with the clouds.

This one is for Sagarika - the girl who laughed, dreamed and, lived. Now, read on.

*

The Unlikely Saviour

By Sagarika

The Characters:

> Momma
> Alicia – The 1st daughter
> Pinky – The 2nd daughter
> Q, short for cutie – The baby
> Ark ('B' silent as per Q) – The dog
> Rambo Remo – The jaywalker

Alien Forcethinkers from the Freecreateworld:

> The Eldest Forcethinker
> The Elder Forcethinker
> The Sujjestor
> Bounce
> Other Forcethinkers
> The Dark Cloud

A faraway world shows luminescent beings. They have no forms and lead a perfect existence. Their thought waves enable them to understand situations. Slowly they begin to detect disturbances around them, very close to their world that could surround and destroy their existence.

Recognizing the danger, they begin to collectively search for a being (of high intelligence in combination with critical tactical abilities) that would help rescue them by offering an enterprising solution. Their search leads them to planet Earth.

Life on Freecreateworld contrasts sharply with life on Earth. Its noise, smells, differently abled beings, their thoughts etc. terrify and disturb the peaceful Forcethinkers. They are upset at the mannerisms and attitude of the humans, the continual damage inflicted on the fragile ecosystem.

Watching people interact in social as well as societal situations amuse them. Thus, coming to recognize the capabilities of the earthly beings through careful observations, they focus on several potential candidates. During this process, they are puzzled by the needs of people for all things mechanical.

Enter Rambo Remo, the jaywalker. This character draws their attention to his goofy ways and they mistakenly assume that this is the savior they have been looking for.

By relating to his needs, they convey their wish. In exchange, they would give him everything that he desires. All this is done via the thought process and during his sleep. Rambo perceives the idea in flashes and initially seems befuddled. The random flashes now begin to accelerate once he begins to selectively piece together the real from the not normal.

NOTE: *The beings do not come to Earth at any point of time. Everything is conveyed via Energized Wave Patterns.*

Finally when danger seems imminent, the youth is asked to retain awareness towards the shift into their world. An energy field is seen moving as a vortex, gaining in strength until BOOM....

The wrong person is transported to Freecreateworld!

It's a woman in her late thirties. Definitely not Rambo Remo.

Both groups are shocked. Eldest Forcethinker and Elder Forcethinker desperately try to reverse the vortex but the gap in the time lapse converge and changes are now irreversible. The Sujjestor who helped pick Rambo Remo is paralyzed with fear. The woman is nonplussed and dazedly looks around after which, she begins to cry. She rants, shrieks and screams abuse at the silent three. Stamping her feet and wailing as though hurt, the woman vents out her shock. The outcry brings all the Forcethinkers into a huddle. Most flinch from the sonic assault on their senses.

Momma (as she is called at home) misses her 3 young ones especially the youngest—lovingly called 'Q'.

The Forcethinkers try to reach out to the mother in a bid to pacify her. To their surprise, they face a blank wall. After several tries, the mother reverses their thoughts back at them, leaving them confounded. They reach out and tentatively share thoughts. Slowly normalcy is achieved. The Eldest Forcethinker and Elder Forcethinker quickly convey the grim situation to the mother who understands their terrible fate but is clueless on how to help. As Momma was not the Forcethinkers' choice, they do not think that she has the potential for devising their escape either. Both parties lose hope and fall silent.

Meanwhile, the Forcethinkers transform themselves into items that they had watched on earth just to make Momma happy. Through their mutual thought pattern, Bounce, a cheerful transformer Forcethinker forms a beautiful flower at first, then, a bright bird, etc. Slowly, Momma's visual clarity attains physical perfection and she enjoys an actual represent-ation of her world. Later, they begin to take on the manifestation of her children and lovable Ark. This makes her happy.

When the black cloud arrives, it envelops the beings and they are converted into frozen luminescent blocks with glowing orbs of light within them. Once it passes them, they are squeezed into nothingness.

As it nears Momma, her infant (one of the Forcethinkers) precedes her as if in defense but the motherly instinct in Momma comes to the fore and she moves quickly to push Q behind her and face the cloud in defiance. The force displays astonishment at first and conveys amusement at the woman's effrontery. Momma is trembling with fear but tells the force fiercely that it should not touch her child or her home.

The air around Momma trembles. The dark cloud senses her desperation and pulls back for the final assault. Momma is now on autopilot mode and allows her instinct to guide her. She reaches out for a volunteer Forcethinker. The one mimicking Ark (Bounce) rushes forward with a happy grin. The tail wagger looks at her trustingly and transforms in an instant into a vacuum ingestor. Both Momma and Bounce understand what is about to happen. A sacrifice has to be made for the common good. Momma requests the injestor to increase itself in size and power. Her heart is heavy yet, she is determined. The machine becomes huge...bigger... giant-sized until the Dark cloud is sucked in!

The Eldest and the Elder Forcethinker along with all other Forcethinkers use their Vortex transporter to shift it to the darkest-place-of-all in the galaxy where it shatters into a million pieces.

The sonic boom and light effect temporarily stuns all. Everyone collapses under the strain. When Momma recovers, she is concerned that her hair is singed.

Momma later indicates her preference to leave, even though she has been offered all the riches of the universe. Her singular thought, is to be back with her family. The Forcethinkers create her image on the planet (in her honor) and help Momma reach home.

The Forcethinkers watch the happy scenes of Momma reuniting with her family. Alicia has taken care of the two younger ones. In reality, only a few hours have passed and the kids are under the assumption that Momma was at the hairdresser's. On entering her room, the flower that the beings created for her the very first time, is seen on her dressing table. Momma touches it and smiles sweetly. She knows that her friends are watching.

~ 167 ~

Endnotes

Remember the time when danger had closed in and the beings were being sucked away into nothingness? Freecreateworld and Momma's visual field had begun to diminish and she had to finally face the harsh truth-to understand that the Forcethinkers were giving her happiness in spite of facing imminent destruction without expecting anything in return. Momma understood then and there that THIS was her family as well and that they all loved each other.

This was when she cleared her mind and requested her few remaining friends to create the visual illusion that contained her home and loved ones. Bounce was to be sacrificed once her plan was put into action but they had to win at any cost. This was her family the dark force was attempting to touch.

'Want war? You got it. This is MY TURF, sweetie. And don't you dare step into it.' The dark cloud took Momma's threat lightly. It did not understand or realize the fact that when a mother faces a crisis that jeopardizes the safety of her family, she goes all out to protect them. And this, she does better than any hero!!

Cheers.

*

GLOSSARY

1. Gramayur, Oothukudi, Koottupuram, Kanhaganj, Ravirajapuram – These are fictitious places created with a view to suit the narrative.
2. Neem – A tree in the mahogony family widely seen in India.
3. Mangifera Indica – Botanical name for the Mango tree.
4. Neelam – A native variety of the Mango fruit commonly available in the South of India.
5. Krithi – A classical composition from the Carnatic school of music.
6. Dakshina – The ancient practice of offering a gift or donation to a Spiritual head or teacher before formal commencement of classes.
7. Kurti – A traditional upper garment worn by Indian women.
8. Veshti – A traditional wraparound garment (for the lower segment) worn by Indian men.
9. Sagu paapaa – Sagu, the little one.
10. Saguma – An affectionate (shortened) version of the name as used by the family members.
11. The Reader's Review – A fictional tabloid.
12. Sabzi – A vegetable dish normally without gravy.
13. Kurinji – Purplish blue flowers that bloom once in twelve years.
14. Zamindar – The Hindi word for landlord.
15. Pannayar – The Thamizh word for Zamindar.
16. Periyaaiyya – Elder + master; the Thamizh word used to respectfully address Sagarika's father.

- Manaiyya – Manav + aiyya
- Periyamma – Elder/Senior + madam/mother
- Doctoramma – Doctor + madam/mother

17. Maariyamman, Vaishno Devi – Different names of the female Godhead as referred to in the South and North of India.
18. Manavlalji – In Hindi, the suffix 'ji' is added to a name to convey respect to the person/hierarchy.
19. Amma – Mother
20. Appa – Father
21. Bindi – A red dot placed between the eyebrows or forehead of Hindu girls and women. It is understood to shelter and protect the third (inner) eye from evil influences.
22. Anjaneya – also known as Hanuman, supreme devotee of Lord Rama.
23. Bhojanalaya – A place where food is served, in other words, a restaurant.
24. Idli – A popular South Indian food item made out of lentils and rice that is ground, fermented and steamed.
25. Rasam – A thin, spicy South Indian soup often mixed and eaten with cooked rice.
26. Athirasam – A delicacy that is made out of jiggery and coarse rice flour, with the added flavor of cardamom.
27. Murukkus – A savory, crunchy snack made out of rice and black gram flour.
28. Thokku – A semi-dry appetizer typically used as a flavor enhancer in South Indian meals.
29. Gongura chutney – A semi-dry appetizer made using the leaves of the red-sorrel.
30. Appalam and Vadagam – Thin, crisp, disc-shaped lentil crackers that are baked or fried and served with Indian meals. Appalams are bigger in size than

vadagams. The latter is normally prepared and sun dried at home.

31. Thali – A meal made up of a selection of dishes that is offered on a platter.

32. Mami – Thamizh word for aunt.

33. Pattumami – The traditional Tamil Brahmin wife decked in the madisaar (9 yard silk saree).

34. Shavaasan – The final pose in a yoga class that allows for deep restoration.

About the Author

Since her formal advent into the field of writing via the Sharjah International Book Fair in 2018, Anitha Padanattil has authored a sci-fi novel for young adults and a biography for young children based on the early life of the Ruler of Sharjah.

Apart from two translations that were worked upon and published the very next year, the author was fortunate to be part of the coveted Guinness World Records held by the SIBF in 2019. The record-breaking event featured 1502 authors simultaneously signing their books at the venue.

Some of her short reads can also be accessed on amazon.in and writers.artoonsinn.com

Anitha Padanattil lives in Dubai with her husband and daughter.